LEARNING CURVE

This is a work of fiction. Names, characters, places and events described herein are products of the author's imagination or are used fictitiously. Any resemblance to actual events, locations, organizations, or persons, living or dead, is entirely coincidental.

Learning Curve

Edited by Sharon Morton Smith

Cover artwork by Craig Jennion (www.craigjennion.com)
Inset artwork by Carol Marschner Malone (www.marschnermalone.com)

Barking Rain Press
PO Box 822674
Vancouver, WA 98682 USA
www.barkingrainpress.org

ISBN Hardcover: 1-935460-99-4
ISBN Paperback: 1-935460-62-5
ISBN eBook: 1-935460-63-3
Library of Congress Control Number: 2013937571

First Edition: September 2013

Printed in the United States of America

9 7 8 1 9 3 5 4 6 0 9 9 2

Maureen —
This is a
very "fun" "escape
"read". love,
B

DEDICATION

To everyone who ever pursued
the Silicon Valley dream.

"Shall I always have to turn away from what surrounds me in order to look for my true place? Must home for me always be in the distance? How should I ever rest, if there is something better? When I see and adopt the better thing, don't I make it mine, don't I prove that it was always mine by divine right? Why should it still seem half foreign and unsatisfying?"

—George Santayana, *The Last Puritan*

"Men rise from one ambition to another: first, they seek to secure themselves against attack, and then they attack others."

—Niccolò Machiavelli, *The Prince*

V. 1.0

D an Crowen, sitting on a stack of equipment boxes, straightened the eight pages of his speech by tapping the paper on his thigh for the fourth time. As he did, he noticed, in the lurid blue glow of the screen beside him, a tiny length of thread on his right sleeve. He picked it off, then smiled at himself: as if anyone will be able to see it.

But then again… He glanced up at the forty-foot-tall canvas screen, the bright red sans serif letters of "Validator Software" written backwards almost two stories above him. Beyond the screen he could hear the low rumble of five hundred conversations, punctuated by the squeaks of chairs and the rattle of male laughter.

"Mr. Crowen?"

Dan turned his head to see a skinny man dressed in black with a slash of black hair across his forehead. "Is it time already?" he asked.

"Yes sir. The hall's almost full." He held out a lavaliere microphone in one hand, battery pack in the other. "You know how to do this, right? Or do you need help?"

Dan took the apparatus. "No, I've got it." He took the battery pack, its little LED glowing red, and reached back and clipped it to his belt—

the expensive Brioni he'd bought in Savile Row on a business trip twenty years before. Dan was amused to suddenly realize that the inexplicably worn area on his belt—that he'd noticed just this morning—had come from two decades of television appearances and public speeches. Then he tucked the wire into his waistband and threaded it up behind the buttons of his shirt. Three buttons up, he pulled the wire out, made a stress loop in the clip behind the microphone, then attached it to his tie—his lucky red tie—a few inches below the half-Windsor knot.

"You've done this before," said the technician. That's what they always said. "May I?" the man asked, reaching into Dan's jacket. He flicked the switch on the battery pack. The little light turned green.

Dan raised his eyebrows and pointed at the tiny black square on his tie. "Don't worry," said the man with emo hair. "You can talk. I've got the pot over there." He pointed to where a heavy-set man sat a control panel. "It's turned all the way down. As you step out on the stage, I'll crank it back up."

A heavy hand landed on Dan's shoulder. "Ready, boss?"

Dan turned to look up into the wide, ferocious grin of his VP of sales, Tony D. "Hey, pal," said Dan, holding out a hand to be gripped in Tony's own. Salesmen always had intense, enveloping handshakes. It was their real calling card.

"Another year, another Homecoming game, eh Dan?" In the near darkness, Tony D.'s perpetually tanned face was a dark orange. But his white teeth almost glowed. "How many has it been?"

"Ten years," said Dan. "We've been doing this for an even decade."

"Holy shit," said Tony D. He whistled. "That many, huh? I had no fucking idea. So where's the champagne and the strippers? We should be *celebrating.*"

Dan nodded and chuckled. Good old Tony D. Outrageous as ever.

The room erupted with the loud click of a microphone like a pistol shot, then the enormous baritone voice of the announcer—a local sports reporter—intoned like the voice of God, "Ladies and Gentlemen! Welcome to the 2010 World Wide Sales Meeting of—" the voice jumped a half-octave even as it swelled in volume. "...Validator Software Incorporated!"

The ballroom, holding every bit of its 1800-person limit, crackled and throbbed with applause and cheers. The backstage area was suddenly awash in color—Dan looked up to see digital fireworks, almost as large as the real thing, exploding around the Validator software above him.

Tony D.'s hand again slapped Dan's shoulder. "Don't worry Dan," he shouted into his ear. "You know I give the best foreplay in the business."

"Break a leg," said Dan, but Tony D. was already sprinting up the steel steps to the waiting stagehand who was holding the curtains.

"...and now," announced the voice, "the Straw that Stirs the Drink. The man-with-the-plan for keeping Validator Number One, the first to arrive and the last to leave at... the hotel bar. The man who sinks the longest putts, tells the dirtiest jokes, drinks the oldest whiskey, and chases the youngest waitresses. And, do I have to say it? The man who writes your annual review—so you damn well better applaud: Your Vice President of Sales... *The Mighty Tony D.!*"

Dan looked up in time to see Tony D. shrug his shoulders and roll his head like a boxer, then nod to the stagehand. The curtain was pulled back, and the brilliant white light turned Tony D. into a silhouette. The crowd, as always, cheered lustily. They had to, of course: it was a matter of cheering themselves on their own success. But Tony D. always got that last ten percent of emotion just from the personal attachment the sales force felt for him. That's why he's the best, Dan thought. Outside of this job, Tony D. is Cosmo's best gift to me.

Dan closed his eyes and listened to the roar washing back and forth across the hall. He just picked up a tiny crackle as the guy at the mixing board pulled up Tony's microphone. Dan pictured Tony pacing the front of the stage, hands in the air, or pointing at familiar faces he could just pick out of the darkened front row.

"Best year ever!" Tony D. shouted. "Best year ever! Because of you! Because of you!"

The roar began to subside. Tony would now be holding his hands out, palms down, slowly bowing with his chin even as he lowered his hands, and with them, the volume of the applause. "Let's get this done!" he shouted. "The bar opens in twenty minutes."

More laughter. But it dampened quickly. Most of the Validator sales force had been with the company for years, and they knew Tony's code for getting his speech underway.

Tony D. began slowly, with a hushed, conspiratorial voice. "So... did we kick ass this year or what?"

Another roar. But now the sound ended quickly. Cheering wasn't nearly as much fun as hearing the next thing Tony had to say.

"Let's see…" Dan glanced up to see a forty-foot-tall Tony D. pull a small notebook out of his jacket pocket and thumb through it.

"Ah, here it is. Record pre-tax revenues. Record after-tax revenues. Record profit margins…" He labored his voice, as if this long recitation of success was exhausting. "… Record profits. Record earnings per share." Tony D. paused, putting a thoughtful finger to his lips. "Hmmm, wasn't there something else?" He theatrically thumbed though the notebook. "Cindy, Mindy, the Pink Poodle Lounge…" The crowd started to chuckle. "…Ah! There it is. Record sales per field office…" The crowd started to cheer. "… Record sales per sales representative… record bonuses…"

The cheers grew louder. Tony D. was starting to shout now. "Record number of new product introductions! Record stock price!" The crowd sounded like it had risen to its feet. "…And best of all, *crushing our competitors' nuts!*"

Dan imagined the crowd jumping up, giving each other high-fives and shouting its encouragement to the energetic man on stage.

The crowd noisily re-seated itself as Tony D. waited. Then, with a calm and measured voice, the Validator vice president of sales said, "You are the best in the business. And I am more proud of you than I can ever say. So instead of talking about it, I'm going to show you how much this company appreciates what you've done. Ladies and gentlemen, hold onto your seats… Here is our new sales commission structure!"

The light around Dan changed from blue to green as an immense slide jumped onto the screen. He lowered his head and returned to his notes. The rest would be sales force insider stuff, punctuated by jokes that wouldn't be quite as crude or funny as in the days when the sales force were all salesmen. Besides, Dan had signed off on all these slides a week ago.

Dan only looked up again when in the background he heard Tony D. say, "But why should you be listening to me about our strategy for the next fiscal year when you can hear it from the man himself?"

That was his cue. Dan jumped to his feet, folded his papers in half, shoved them into his jacket pocket, and trotted up the stairs to the stage. The stagehand was there, waiting. As Dan stepped up, the stagehand reached down and, as respectfully as he could with the CEO of one of his largest clients, gently pulled open Dan's jacket to confirm that the red light on the battery pack had switched to green. He pointed at the microphone on Dan's tie and then at his own ear. Dan nodded in understanding.

Tony D's voice was slowly rising. "… I don't have to tell you what this man has done for Validator Software—what he has done for *you*—in his ten years at the head of this company. Cosmo Validator is the heart of this company, but this man is the brains. Brilliant, strategic, a born leader, and a man of honor and integrity. He's the reason Validator is the best place to work in Silicon Valley. And he'd be a killer poker player if he wasn't so goddamned honest. Ladies and gentlemen, the worst bluffer in the world, but a helluva Chief Executive. My boss and my friend, *Mr. Dan Crowen!*"

Dan glanced up to see an image of himself thirty feet taller and five years younger than the real thing. The curtain pulled open before him, and he stepped out into the intense light, trying not to squint. He held up a hand to wave, and then headed for the podium to his right, where Tony D. still stood pointing towards him. They gave each other a public handshake and forearm grip while—cognizant of his open mike—Dan smiled and nodded. But Tony leaned in and whispered in Dan's ear, "They're wet and ready for you, big guy," winked, and left the stage.

Shaking his head—the crowd saw his response and laughed heartily— Dan stepped behind the podium, then pulled the papers out of his jacket and straightened them on its top. He looked out on the crowd. His eyes now more adjusted, Dan could see that the crowd was on its feet. He'd long ago realized that praise was merely part of being a CEO, but he was nonetheless gratified by its duration. He remembered how abbreviated the Standing-O had been those first couple years when the company was struggling and the economy was weak.

He nodded and mouthed his thank-yous, all while listening for that first dip in volume that was a signal. There it was. "Good afternoon, everyone," he projected over the fading applause. "It's been a great year for Validator Software. Indeed, it has been the best year in our company's thirty-year history. And much of the credit for that success goes to *you*."

The sales force was back on its feet. *Eight minutes,* Dan told himself. *Talk, don't read. Look up. Keep the rhythm going. Work the finish hard.*

"Our… *irrepressible* friend, Mr. Tony D., has been good enough to list all of the incredible things that you have accomplished in the last year. I know that the rest of the company—marketing, manufacturing, admin, finance— is incredibly proud of what you've done… just as I am sure that you are equally proud to work with them."

There was a murmur of assent from the crowd. "At Validator Software, we are a family," Dan continued. "We are a team. We are together no matter where we find ourselves in the world. And that, more than new products or new sales and marketing campaigns, is the real reason why we win. Why we are number one."

The applause was growing. "It's why we will stay Number One next year. And the year after that. And the year after that!"

A roar rushed up to him, and Dan lowered his voice to make it more intimate. He knew he wasn't Tony D.—but he didn't have to be. "We did great things, historic things, this year. But now that's history. The new year will bring new challenges, new opportunities, and maybe even new competitors. We have to be ready for all of them. Are you ready?"

"Yes!" shouted the Validator sales force.

"You know what? I already knew that. Because I already knew that you are the best in the business. Otherwise, why would you be part of the best company in the industry?"

The applause was deafening, and Dan was caught up in it himself. "But even the best need the right products to sell, the right sales tools, and the right marketing and advertising support to be all it can be. So…" Dan looked suspiciously left and right. "Any spies here from CMR or Twillium?"

A chorus of boos echoed in the auditorium. "Good," said Dan conspiratorially. "Because I know I can trust you—"

"You bet!" someone shouted back.

"Let me give you an early glimpse of what we have coming your way over the next twelve months…"

Six minutes later it was over. The crowd took to its feet in applause. Dan smiled, made a brief wave, and headed to the front of the stage, where he bent down, said hello, and shook hands with every salesperson—some old friends and veterans, some newcomers trying to be remembered, a few attempting to blurt out the contents of a long-ignored memo. He dealt graciously but quickly with them all. He was soon joined by Tony D., who was his usually gregarious and profane self, but whose very presence made the crowed quickly shrink away—just as he'd planned.

As they walked back through the curtains, Tony D. slapped Dan on the back. "That's the bread and circuses for this year. Doing the usual 'quiet dinner with the missus' thing tonight?"

"Yep."

"Well," said Tony D. as they stepped off the stairs, "I suppose you need to be fresh and alert and all of that other bullshit for tomorrow. But as for me, I'm going to celebrate one great fucking year. Maybe that's why you're the CEO and I'm not."

"That must be it," said Dan with a tired smile.

The stagehand was waiting to take the microphones, carefully coiling each to keep them from tangling. "Terrific job, gentlemen," he said.

Dan glanced up and saw a familiar figure threading her way through the packing crates and cables. It was his secretary, Donna, cradling a pile of papers and portfolios against her hip in her sleeved arm. She always wore a long-sleeved blouse to cover some unwelcome tattoos from her past—not an unusual sight back at corporate headquarters, but odd here. He couldn't ever remember Donna coming to one of these sales speeches. This wasn't good.

"Dan," she said breathlessly as she arrived. Her face was flushed, as if she'd been running. "You aren't going to like this."

"Okay." he said evenly.

"Mr. Validator called. He wants to talk with you."

"I'll call him once I get outside."

"In person."

"Oh. All right. Fine. Where's he staying?"

"In Idaho. At the ranch."

"No. He's kidding, right?"

Donna just pressed her lips together in reply. "Mr. Validator's plane is waiting at the San Jose Jetport. It's fueled up, the crew's on, and it's ready to go when you are. I have a car and driver waiting outside."

"Cosmo wants me to fly all the way to Idaho for a five minute meeting and fly all the way back tonight?" He glanced at his watch. "It's already 3:30, for God sakes."

"No sir. He wants you to fly back there this evening, and then get up early to meet him in the morning. You'll then fly back together to the shareholders meeting." She motioned down at the stack of papers. "These are all of the documents you'll need for tomorrow and the meeting."

Dan's shoulders slumped. "Did he say why?"

"No. I heard everything from some new assistant he has. She wasn't very friendly. I've told you everything she told me."

"I'll need a change of clothes and my medicine kit."

"Already taken care of. Along with some casual clothes in case you want to walk around the ranch. And I've told Ms. Crowen. She also picked out your suit and tie for the meeting tomorrow. The driver has already stopped by your house and they're waiting in the car."

"Thank you. How did Annabelle sound?"

"At least as disappointed as you."

He nodded. "Well. It's got to be done." He reached out and took the papers. "Thanks for taking care of everything, Donna."

"Sure, Dan. And I'm very sorry. I know these evenings are very important."

Dan gave her a wan smile. "See you tomorrow."

As the limousine made its way down the commute lane on Highway 280, past the gridlock of cars in the other lane, Dan pulled out his Blackberry and called home. His wife answered after a single ring.

"Don't worry," she said peremptorily. "Dinner can wait."

"I know, but it won't be the same dinner. I mean, this is our own private tradition. And I don't know about you, but I'm hugely disappointed. The prospect of a quiet evening together. A nice dinner and an expensive bottle of wine. Aiden at a friend's house. Coffee on the patio. A little fun. A real honest-to-god good night's sleep. It's the prospect of it all that gets me through this miserable week every year."

"I know, honey. And I'm disappointed too. If you had cancelled for any other reason, you know I'd be furious. But this is Cosmo. And Cosmo is crazy. He's always been crazy. And he has no concept that other people have lives. That's why you had to save his company. He worked his people nearly to death, until they quit, and then took all the credit for the company's success. I figured out a long time ago that bitching about Cosmo Validator is like complaining about earthquakes—it doesn't do a lick of good. You either move away or deal with it, but you can't fight it. He loves you, dear."

"Yeah, lucky me. And lucky you I'm not twenty years younger, because that's more his style."

"Tomorrow night?"

"Aiden will love it. Two overnights in a row? That's her idea of paradise. Besides, the filets and the zin will be just that much more aged."

"I like the way you think."

"Thanks. Try at least to get a good night's sleep. At least you've already done the heavy lifting. All you have to do tomorrow is shake hands and look presidential." Dan smiled; after all these years, Annabelle knows my job as well as I do. Smarter than me, too.

"Maybe I'll keep the cowboy gear on," he said. The shareholders would love it."

"Why not? I'm sure Cosmo's done it before."

Dan chuckled. "I'll call you later."

"Safe trip," said Annabelle. "Love you."

V. 1.1

The limousine pulled up to the electric gate at the side of the terminal. The driver handed a piece of paper to the guard, who nodded and returned to his booth. With a shudder, the gate rattled open and they drove through—past the open front of the hangar with its parked collection of private jets, and out onto the edge of the flight line. Cosmo Validator's Bombardier was waiting just ahead, turbines slowly turning. Skirting the horizontal stabilizer, the car pulled up at the base of the plane's lowered steps. "Thanks," said Dan. "You're picking me up tomorrow."

"Yes sir," said the driver. "Do you know when yet?"

"I know nothing," said Dan. "But someone will let you know."

He opened the door, and with just two steps on the tarmac, he was on the step-up into the plane. The flight attendant, a stunning brunette—Validator never had anything less—greeted him as he entered. "Mr. Crowen. Welcome aboard. It's been a while, hasn't it? Davos, three years ago."

"Yes. Yes, I remember. It's good to see you again, Wendy."

"Would you like a glass of wine before we take off?"

"That would be fine."

"We have no other passengers, Mr. Crowen, so please make yourself comfortable anywhere."

Dan knew that meant Validator would not be on the flight. And that, in turn, meant that Cosmo's designated seat—the one in the center near the rear bulkhead, with kidskin upholstery and its own special control panel—was available. Dan decided instead to take a window seat.

He sipped his wine and watched the limousine driver unload his suitcase and suiter and hand it up the steps. He looked out across the airport to the swooping stainless steel walls of the new Mineta Airport, looking like some great vacuum cleaner against the distant skyline of downtown San Jose. A Southwest Air 737 was taxiing out for take-off, a face in every window. Dan gave a small smile: that would normally be him, enjoying the modest advantages of business class, and thankful for them all. That's how CEOs travelled—at least until they made the Fortune 500 and the company bought a plane. Only founders could afford their own jets.

"Mr. Crowen?"

Dan looked up to see the pilot—there'd be two of them—in his uniform without the jacket.

"Welcome back. If you are ready sir, we have clearance from the tower."

"By all means," said Dan.

"Very good. Your choice, Mr. Crowen, but we do prefer that you buckle your seatbelt."

"Of course."

The pilot made a casual two finger salute. "I'll check back with you somewhere over Nevada."

Dan looked across the aisle and out the far window. The sun, the color of butter, was resting above Swig tower at Santa Clara University, and preparing to dive behind the wave of fog cresting over the distant Santa Cruz Mountains. The Jesuits had given him an honorary degree two years before; the diploma now hung on the wall of his home office. *It'll be dark in Idaho when we land,* he told himself.

There was no shuddering, bouncing, or rattling, just a whine of the engine and an infinitesimal diminution of vibration as the Bombardier leapt off the runway and hurtled into the air. Dan felt the G's slightly as the plane made a tighter bank than a commercial airplane, but it wasn't enough to do much more than slightly tilt the wine in his glass. After a few minutes, the plane crested the eastern hills, with the ranger station atop Mt. Diablo surprisingly close off the left wing. As the golden light flickered off the Bay and spires of San Francisco, the flight attendant appeared in the aisle ahead and began opening cabinets. She was gorgeous. That's what all stewardesses looked like when I was a boy, Dan told himself. Now rich men keep them for themselves.

He closed his eyes; he was surprised to feel how quickly he was breathing. Was it residual adrenalin from the speech? The change of plans? Or the impending meeting with Cosmo? Probably all of them. But probably the last most of all.

Odd, how our roles have reversed, he mused. Cosmo was born in Redwood City—a fourth generation Californian whose ancestor had proved a better fisherman than gold miner—and a man more Silicon Valley than Silicon

Valley itself. Yet Cosmo now lived on a 33,000-acre ranch in Idaho, and treated the Valley like a strange and alien landscape that he occasionally had to visit but couldn't escape quickly enough. Meanwhile, Dan realized, here I am, the son of a Back Bay Boston grocer who bleeds Dartmouth green, and I never travelled west of the Berkshires until I was sixteen years old. Now, the instant the wheels touch off the runway I feel an ache of homesickness to be back in the Valley.

He had begun his career at an investment banking firm in Manhattan. For fifteen years—beginning the Monday after his MBA graduation from Tuck—he had worked his way up through the ranks to the top floor, and became a partner. He was supposed to stay there forever. He'd already gone from young buck to newlywed to new father, and from the walk-up in Chelsea to the apartment off Columbus Circle to the house in Garden City. Circling and circling in an ever-upward gyre—Connecticut next, and then back to the city. Senior partner, then chairman. It was so predictable and perfect. Set your clock; set your calendar—the road ahead was smooth and well-marked.

And then Cosmo Validator showed up one day and shattered it all.

It hadn't begun that way, of course. Validator Software was just one more of those hot tech companies out West, full of engineers and scientists who didn't know how to buy a suit or order a meal but had a native genius for making fortunes. Dan barely understood what half of them did—Validator, for example, made (manufactured? wrote?) something called 'productivity software,' which seemed to have almost nothing to do with any notion of productivity he'd ever learned in business school.

But it didn't matter. All that counted was that the marketplace wanted these new products, and the stock market wanted to own pieces of these new companies. And so these California companies—from a place called 'Silicon Valley' that seemed to be located south of San Francisco and near Stanford but had no recognizable landmarks, buildings, or even topographic features—found a way to grow more quickly than any companies in history… and make money with astonishing speed.

But it took money—a lot of money—to make money at this rate. And these little Silicon Valley start-ups, despite paying their employees with as much stock as cash, and despite never paying dividends to shareholders, were insatiable when it came to capital. Chip companies, consumer electronics companies, even software companies never seemed to have enough money to invest in their own operations. With the semiconductor companies, like Intel, this was understandable—their fabrication laboratories were like something out of NASA. And the consumer electronics and computer game folks like Apple and Atari needed factories able to absorb millions of orders.

But why, Dan had regularly asked himself at the time, did software companies need so much money? All they sold was a bunch of bits on computer disks; how much could that cost? It would be years—truth be told, only after he joined Validator Software—before he finally appreciated the financial dynamics of software: the overhead of superstar code writers, the heavy investment in marketing and advertising to capture market share, and the short product life cycle between upgrades.

That education began seventeen years before, on the day Cosmo Validator walked into the bank. His hair was darker then—it was not yet the great silver mane that would become his most indelible image—but still shocking for a corporate CEO. And even then he wore bespoke suits and cowboy boots on his 6 foot 5 inch frame.

Those who saw him arrive never forgot it. Silicon Valley tycoons were still not a common sight in the canyons of Wall Street, and when Validator stepped out of a limousine and strode towards the glass doors, even jaded New Yorkers froze on the sidewalk to let him pass. He had the same effect upon the poor receptionist. She had handled heads of state with aplomb, but this incarnation of pure Alpha Entrepreneur seemed to paralyze her into speechlessness.

Validator waited a full fifteen seconds, staring without moving at the sputtering receptionist, then finally said in what could only be described as a booming whisper, "Little girl, if you can't speak, then at least hold up the correct number of fingers to tell me what floor the Underwriting department is on."

She finally managed to tell him. "May I tell them who's calling?"

But Validator was already gone. The terrified receptionist tried to call ahead, but that department was preoccupied with a small birthday celebration… for Dan Crowen. The phone was still ringing and the office staff singing 'Happy Birthday' when Cosmo Validator slammed through the glass doors and surveyed the scene. Standing with his hands on his hips, he announced, "Well, goddamnit, if this isn't *exactly* how we Californians figure you all spend your workday."

There was a quick scramble of secretaries, clerks, and even partners, and Validator was hurriedly led into the conference room. As the lead associates on the Validator Software account raced to their offices to gather up the requisite paperwork, Dan found himself alone across the table from the new arrival. Cosmo leaned back in his chair, checked his nails, and then began to stare at the young man. "What's your name, kid?"

In those days, when he was still uncertain that he had earned his place in the world, encountering one of the most extraordinary human beings he'd ever seen would normally have made Dan Crowen duck away from making eye contact and hurry to escape any conversation. But at this moment, he was pissed off enough about this inexcusable and rude interruption of his party that he looked the older man right in the eye and said, "Daniel Crowen, associate on your account."

"Ah," said Cosmo Validator. "Having a happy birthday, Mr. Crowen? What is it: your twenty-fifth? Twenty-sixth?"

"Thirty-seventh," said Dan firmly. "And I was having a good one until you crashed my party."

Validator stared at him for a long moment—until Dan was convinced the man was going to leap across the table and throttle him—then burst into hearty laughter.

"Well, shit. I guess I did, didn't I? Did you even get some of your own cake?"

"No."

Validator slapped the table. "We can't have that, now can we?" He jumped to his feet—for such a towering man, he was remarkably nimble—and headed for the door. Dan sat up in disbelief. Validator flung open the door and shouted, "Everybody! The party isn't over. All of you, get in here. And somebody bring the goddamn cake!"

Two minutes later, the entire Underwriting department was crowded into the conference room, singing 'Happy Birthday,' heartily led by Cosmo Validator—who had already managed to forget Dan's name... and substituted 'The Kid.'

His office mates were still calling Dan 'The Kid' four years later when he left for California.

After that, the meeting would have been anti-climactic but for two things. First, it began to dawn on everyone in the room that the Validator initial public offering (for that was why Cosmo had come to New York) might be one of the biggest tech IPOs in history—perhaps even rivaling Netscape a few years before, and Apple Computer before that. In fact, in the end, Validator's Going Public Day would not quite reach those exalted heights—but it would be the biggest software company IPO in history.

The second reason the meeting was so memorable was that when the discussion turned to the international road show that Validator and part of his management team would have to embark upon in the final weeks before Going Public Day, Cosmo—who had turned half away from the table to stare out at the Manhattan skyline—suddenly spun back and around. He looked at each of the men facing him—then pointed at Dan and said, "I'd like The Kid to come along on the tour." He winked at Dan and added, "It'll be one long birthday party."

In fact, it was more like the world's most expensive bachelor party. Each day was spent in taxis, racing through some capital city of Europe or Asia on the way to the fifth or sixth presentation of the day; each night was burned on an expensive dinner in an elegant restaurant and a quick stop in a strip club or bar, followed by a red-eye flight to the next country. Tokyo (geishas), Hong Kong (scary food and endless booze), Paris (sex shows), London (dinner with the Chancellor of the Exchequer), Johannesburg (liquor), Buenos Aires (chiracurra), Los Angeles (strippers), Seattle (a seedy bar down at the port), San Francisco (drag show), Chicago (they had switched to a leased jet now, and left Dan to sleep in it), and back to New York.

Along the way they had lost two of Validator's employees, who'd had to figure out how to catch up with the team. One had to pay a fine to get out of jail and flew home to Palo Alto; the other showed up two weeks later without a coherent explanation of what had happened. Meanwhile, the rest of the team had been in a crash in a Hong Kong taxi, had talked their way out of a drunk and disorderly arrest in The Hague and, in Dan's case, got food poisoning in Singapore from (drunkenly) eating a fried tarantula on a dare.

In retrospect, the whole trip was a blur, a collection of uncollated mental snapshots without a narrative, only an itinerary. But one recurring memory was vivid: it was of Cosmo Validator, never tired, never flustered, and never out of place—whether he was addressing a group of high-powered institutional investors in London on just two hours sleep, or paying off a customs agent in Seoul, or ordering an unwelcome lap dance for Dan in an LA gentleman's club. There was something about Cosmo Validator—something Dan would find in lesser measure in other famous entrepreneurs—that made him different from other people.

It wasn't just that he was smarter, or even that he seemed to have superhuman levels of energy; most CEOs had those traits. No, it was as if Validator were *wired* differently from other mortals, that he approached the world along a different track, dealt with risk and adversity and failure—even normal relationships—from the opposite perspective that other human beings saw. In the years that followed, Dan would learn to better understand the form of these traits in Cosmo Validator—and see them in other great entrepreneurs—but he would never fully comprehend their nature. So he comforted himself during trying times with Cosmo by rehashing his theory that pure, native entrepreneurs—like sociopaths—might be part of the human population, but they were not necessarily *of* it.

It had taken Dan a month to recover from that road show. He still had a scar on his shin from a taxi door that had been slammed on his leg in Berlin. But the crazy road show quickly became the source of endless stories and anecdotes with which he could regale friends and family. And the interest in those stories only grew as Cosmo Validator metamorphosed from a regional curiosity to a national business superstar to an industry legend. Even now, though he had grown jaded to it, at least once a week, someone he met—often a famous business figure himself—would lean a little closer and ask him, "What's Validator really like?" He had long since learned to reply, "Everything you've ever heard of and a lot more." That reply even had the advantage of being true.

And Dan understood the curiosity. In the years that followed the road show, he found himself increasingly obsessed with Cosmo Validator. Sure, he had other interesting clients—and as he rose through the ranks of the Underwriting department, those clients grew ever-richer, more powerful, and more famous—but none were as interesting as Validator. He wasn't alone in his fascination, and the endless stream of cover stories and features about Cosmo in the *Wall Street Journal, Forbes, Fortune,* and *Business Week* barely slaked Dan's interest in the man.

Everybody knew the Cosmo Validator legend now. The father who'd been a Redwood City fireman until he died in a collapsing warehouse. The protective but unstable mother. The young hood, regularly arrested for drag racing on the El Camino Real... and the now-famous mug shot of a seventeen-year-old "Carl" Validator with a duck ass greaser haircut and a cigarette dangling from his lips. The genius-in-the-rough who aced his SATs and earned a scholarship to Stanford, only to be thrown out for reasons that were in still-sealed records. And the patent that Cosmo filed just a month before being expelled that would ultimately earn Stanford $100 million... and would one day lead the University to give Cosmo an honorary doctorate and name an engineering building after him. And finally, of course, there was the historic Validator Software IPO and the singular road show before it that was reported to have been just this side of a Led Zeppelin tour.

That last only seemed to burnish Dan's own reputation. He increasingly found himself pitching clients by dropping anecdotes about "my friend Cosmo." If pressed further about details, he would just wink and say, "I've got stories about him and me that I don't even tell my wife. But if I talked about Cosmo out of school, how would you trust me to keep *your* secrets?" It worked, too. There were days when Dan felt trapped inside the Cosmo Validator reality distortion zone... and days when he loved every moment of being there.

As for personal contact with Validator, there was very little in the years that followed. An occasional message from Cosmo's assistant, a couple of telephone calls (about which Dan could recount every word), and one cocktail party when Dan had barely a moment to reach through a flock of well-wishers and shake Validator's hand.

But then, three years almost to the day after the IPO, Dan picked up the phone to hear a familiar voice. "Birthday Boy! They say you've come up in the world and now I'm supposed to talk to you. Okay, here's the deal: I've got some big plans brewing, and I'm going to need a secondary offering. If you want it, it's yours."

And so began Dan's second adventure with Cosmo Validator. There was no banzai road show this time, just a few presentations on Wall Street and in San Francisco. But that still meant a week of lunches and dinners (and a couple breakfasts) with Validator, who regaled his audiences of stock analysts with tales of Alaskan bear hunts—one of which nearly killed him—African safaris completing his Big Five, a night with a well-known movie star with unusual proclivities, a night in a Bulgarian jail after running over a drunk who was sleeping on the road, and a drunken late night session in the Ritz bar with the president of France. This time, Dan came away with even more stories to tell, both because he actually slept at night, and also because this time he knew what he was getting into. That said, he found himself secretly disappointed that there were no surprises. He didn't even admit it to Annabelle—though, knowing her, she already knew—but Dan felt more alive in the orbit of Cosmo Validator than he did anywhere else.

He should have known better. Four months after the successful offering, Cosmo Validator called one more time. This time there was no larger-than-life personality on the other end of the line, no reference to birthday boy, only a collection of carefully measured words, no doubt written by an attorney, whose meaning was designed to be legally clear: "Dan, I'd like to offer you the position of Executive Vice-President at Validator Software." Then, as if reading off a prepared script, Cosmo read the duties, salary, and stock options and other perquisites of the position.

Dan had come to expect the unexpected from Validator; but this time he was dumbstruck. Finally, he managed to say, "I'm sorry, Cosmo, but I don't understand. I'm a banker, not a software guy. And you want to put *your* company in *my* hands? What do I know about software?"

Only now did Validator go off script. "Aw, for shit's sake, Dan. What does *anybody* know about software? It's just a bunch of fucking lines of code. And you get a bunch of really smart code writers to write them. That's it. And you don't even have to worry about that, because I know who all the great code writers are… and I hire them.

"No, what this industry needs right now—what *I* need—is smart financial management and disciplined operations. Nobody else seems to have noticed it, but our industry is moving into a new phase. It's not going to be about big-time, game-changing innovation anymore… well, at least not for a long time… but about holding onto what you've got, consolidating markets and customers, cutting costs a little more every year. That and marketing. Great fucking marketing, like the kind that Apple's doing in computers and Intel in semiconductors. We don't know a goddamn thing about any of that stuff. You do."

"A lot of people do," said Dan. "A lot of them more than me."

"Maybe," said Cosmo. "But I know you. You're family. And I trust you."

I am? Dan thought. *You do?*

Three weeks later, he and Annabelle were living in an apartment in Sunnyvale, signing up Aiden for pre-K at a local private school, and looking for an Eichler to buy so they could live the full glass-house and atrium California lifestyle. Looking back, what happened in those three weeks was almost as much of a blur as the Validator road show had been.

It was almost as if the deal had been done without him—and that Dan was the last to know. Apparently, Cosmo had already talked with the chairman of the bank, and the two men had already agreed that while Dan's departure would be a loss for the firm, that sacrifice was worth the reward of having Validator as a guaranteed client in perpetuity. The Underwriting department head, Dan's boss, also knew about it before he did, and had already found Dan's replacement. The going away party had already been reserved that morning at a local restaurant by his secretary for ten days hence, HR had already begun preparing the paperwork… and even Annabelle knew when he arrived home that night, having been called by Validator that afternoon.

It was like the most genteel firing imaginable: Dan was kicked out of one company to tears and congratulatory handshakes by the very people firing him, and instantly catapulted into another job with more power, more money, and more fame. And all he had to do was not say no.

And he didn't. He didn't even have time to hesitate. Dan Crowen's jump to Validator Software did not go unnoticed by either Silicon Valley or Manhattan. The tech media, long accustomed to Cosmo's mercurial hirings and strategic moves, once again asked a question as old as the industry itself: Could an Old World finance guy ever really adapt to the wildcatter lifestyle of the Valley? And, of course, they repeated Dan's own question: "What does this bean counter know about processors, compilers, and writing code?" Dan found himself compared to John Sculley and other traditional industry types who had sailed into Silicon Valley with flags flying... only to be dashed by waves against the rocks. Those publications would ask the same question at each of Dan's promotions in the years that followed, especially when he was appointed President and CEO. It was only after he had been five years in the top job—almost a decade after his arrival in the Valley—that those questions finally faded.

The financial press, as was its style, took a different tack. How, it asked, could these two almost polar opposite personalities ever find enough common ground to work together? *Fortune* even entitled its feature on the piece, "Street Tough meets Eagle Scout," playing on their very different backgrounds. *Business Week* gave the "marriage" six months, predicting that Crowen, tail between his legs, would run back to Wall Street just in time to handle the next Validator stock offering.

Those doubts faded just about the time that Dan himself began to wonder if they were valid.

An elegant hand lightly squeezed his shoulder. "Mr. Crowen?"

Dan looked up to see the pretty flight attendant, silhouetted in the dim light of the cabin. It was already dark outside.

"Sir, the pilot tells me that there is a particularly lovely aurora borealis above us right now. Mr. Validator always likes for his flight guests to see it."

V. 1.2

N ot a hint of sunset glow remained on the western horizon when the plane touched down lightly at Coeur d'Alene Airport, turned away from the terminal, and taxied over to Validator's private hangar. The hangar doors were open, showing a vintage Bell helicopter parked inside. In front of the doors, silhouetted in the bright light from the open hanger, was a Lincoln Navigator with a man in a cowboy hat, his arms folded, standing beside it.

Before the plane's passenger door even opened, the man trotted over to the rear of the plane, unloaded Dan's bags, and began lugging them back to the SUV. And he was there to meet Dan as he stepped down the stairs.

Dan pumped a calloused hand. "Virgil, great to see you. How are you?"

Virgil Mason, the top hand at Validator Ranch, took off his hat, ducked his head, and nodded. "I'm good, Mr. Crowen. It's good to see you, too. It's been a long time."

Dan slapped the man on the back. "It sure has. A couple years at least. Long enough for you to forget to call me Dan."

"Yeah, Dan, I guess it has. Are you ready to go, or do you need to stop for anything?"

"No, let's get going."

"Good. Because Mary's cooking up a nice supper for you."

It was a moonless night, and cloudy. As they turned north on Highway 95, Dan could just make out a few lights beyond the reflection of the dashboard on the passenger window.

"So, Virgil, give me the news. How was hunting this year? Get your elk?"

"Yes sir, got my tags. Shot me a pretty nice one in the National Forest, just south of the lake. It'd been super cold the week before, then started to warm up. Guess he decided to get out and feel the sun on his back."

"Bad choice."

"For him, yeah. But we're still eating the meat."

"Anything new at the ranch?"

"Some new fencing. Painted a couple of the older buildings. That's about it… well, except for the new wife."

"How's that working out?"

Dan glanced over to see that Virgil had pursed his lips, as if trying to figure how much, or how little, to say.

"Ah," said Dan.

"No, no. She's alright, I guess. Just a little different from the other ones."

"What's her name again?"

"Amber. But we never get to call her that. It's always 'Mrs. Validator.'"

"I see. I heard she was a cocktail waitress in Vegas when Cosmo met her."

"That's what I heard, too. But no one talks about that."

"I'm not surprised. So, what's she like? Pretty rough around the edges, eh?"

"No, not as much as you might think. The stuff she buys is pretty nice, at least by my tastes, which ain't much. No, I don't know. I guess you'd say she's… got a lot of energy. She's very ambitious. Very into the whole society thing. She's gotten real heavy with the Republican party around here lately."

Dan chuckled. "The hell you say."

"It keeps her real busy in the evening going to all of these events and glad-handing everybody. Trying to build support, or something like that. Anyway, it keeps her away from the ranch most evenings."

"Well, that's gotta be news," said Dan.

Virgil didn't reply.

"Does she keep Cosmo happy?"

"If she didn't," Virgil replied, "she'd already be gone. Like the other ones."

They crossed over Lake Pend Oreille and passed through Sandpoint. On a long, empty stretch of highway, the truck ran alongside a stretch of expensive new steel fence. After five miles of this, a groomed gravel road turned off to the right. Virgil took the turn and quickly skidded to a halt in front of a huge steel gate under a skeletal arch bearing a cursive 'VR.' He rolled down the window, letting in a blast of chilly air, then reached out and tapped in the entry code on a freestanding keyboard. The gates silently opened.

With the gravel now grinding under the wheels, they set off on a five-mile road that curved over the near ridge. Dan could just make out a faint glow beyond its summit. "Where I live," he said, "my hundred foot driveway is considered long."

"Yeah, heh, I suppose," said Virgil. "This one's long even by Idaho standards."

"Any problem with the Nazis and the Aryan Army these days?"

"Naw. They mostly keep to themselves. Sheriff raids them once in a while on weapons, but that's about it. But I gotta do some serious background checks on anybody who applies for a job on the ranch. Every once in a while, one of those crazies tries to find work near their camp, so I always got to be careful. Actually, poaching is a bigger problem. Lost a couple nice elk last year, and a big mulie. Rangers caught one guy, but they're still looking for the other one."

Just then a huge four-legged form, almost white in the glare of the head-lights, bolted across the road just ahead of them. Virgil involuntarily jerked the wheel, then corrected himself. "Shit."

"Speaking of elk," said Dan.

"Big one, too. Always a risk driving at night this time of year. Like I told you before, Dan, you oughta get up here during the season and cull one of your own. Get Mr. V. to invite you. You can damn near shoot a Boone and Crockett mulie off the back porch. And I'll drive you up in the mountains over there and you'll get a monster elk."

"We'll see," said Dan. "Maybe after my life quiets down. So, how much property does Cosmo own these days?"

"About the same. Picked up a couple small ranches last year. So, he's up to something like 45,000 acres, give or take a few hundred."

"It's hard to picture. I've looked on a map and the house is only like twenty percent into the property."

"Yeah, that's about right. Basically it's everything you see right now—or you would see if it was daylight—all the way out to the mountains out there. And then a few miles into them."

"And you've got to manage every single one of them."

"Yep," said Virgil, "every one."

As the truck crested the ridge, the great house, as bright as a refinery—and nearly as big—at last came into view. "I've never asked," said Dan, "but what's the power bill on that place every month?"

"You don't want to know," said Virgil.

They parked at the foot of the slate walkway leading to the huge copper entrance doors of the four-story river stone and cedar main hall. Through the tall craftsman windows beneath the copper roof, Dan could make out the towering, fifty-foot cedar tree trunks that served as columns. Virgil unloaded Dan's luggage and started towards the doors, but Dan insisted on taking it himself so Virgil could park the truck.

Suitcase and briefcase in one hand and suit bag slung over his shoulder, Dan was just reaching for the doorbell when one of the big doors swung open silently. Mary Mason, Virgil's wife and chief cook for the ranch house, wrapped him in her arms. She was all curves and encased in denim, rhinestone glasses perched on top of her teased hair. The hug lasted a long time. Finally, Mary stepped back, taking the briefcase from Dan's fingers, and gave him the huge, warm smile that was her trademark. "Well, look at you, stranger. About time you paid us a visit."

"I must confess, Mary, that four hours ago I didn't know I was going to be here."

"Oh, honey, I knew that. Do you think *anybody* comes here unannounced? C'mon in."

Before they crossed the threshold, Dan caught Mary's shoulder and whispered, "Where's the great man?"

"Oh," she said in a normal voice, "didn't they tell you? Mr. Validator isn't here. He's flying in from Europe in the morning." Seeing the stricken look on Dan's face, Mary patted him on the chest. "I know, baby, but don't worry. We'll have nice fun evening, just the three of us. And I've got a helluva dinner planned."

Dan made his way across the vast hall. It was almost sixty feet tall at its peak; its distant cedar beams rested atop the great barkless cedar trunks whose own bases were five feet in diameter. There was a fire in the giant fireplace, its mouth tall enough to walk into, and the chimney was a four-story waterfall of rounded river stones, the ones at the base larger than the span of Dan's arms. The flames produced half the light in the room; the rest came from the soft warm glow of van Erp and Tiffany lamps and sconces. Those yellow lights made a soft glow on Persian carpets, on the hammered copper and golden oak of Stickley furniture, and on Remington and Russell bronzes. The flames and light reflected off the distant wall of glass that, during the day, was filled with a panorama of the nearby mountains.

He passed down the long hallway, which was lined with Santa Fe chests and antler and horn chairs and benches. His room, the suite at the end of the hall, was already lit, its doors opened, a fire burning in its own vintage iron stove. This was the "Cowboy Beaux Arts" suite. It had a big brass bed, a hand-painted Victorian bureau and armoire, framed shadow boxes filled with dime novels, and a wall-sized display of Winchester lever action rifles. The curtains were open. By the light of the room, Dan could just make out the statue of The End of the Trail. It was one of Fraser's first run of bronzes—Cosmo had seen it at Sotheby's and paid a fortune "to bring it back West where it belongs." The slumped Indian atop the weary horse was even more evocative in the wintertime, when it stood alone in the snow, fading into the gloom.

Five minutes later, having dumped his suitcase on the bed and hung up his tie, suit, and shirt, Dan was back in the Great Hall. Virgil was waiting for him, sitting on one of the hand-tooled leather couches. A martini and a bowl of cashews stood on the coffee table opposite.

"Bombay Sapphire, anchovy olive, right?" asked Virgil.

Dan dropped heavily onto the couch. "You remembered that after two years?"

"Naah." Virgil made a typing gesture with his fingers. "Database in the bar's computer."

"Of course." Dan raised his glass in a toast. "Good hunting."

"Straight shooting," Virgil replied and took a swig out of his beer glass.

After they finished their drinks, they made their way to the dining room. Its walls were manzanita and glowed deeply with rubbed beeswax, and from the ceiling hung a chandelier made of deer antlers. The two men sat at one end of the antique vestry table with ancient silver conchas nailed around its perimeter. Mary arrived a moment later, carrying a plate and followed by two assistants, one with two more plates and the other carrying a silver lidded casserole.

Mary set the plate in front of Dan.

"Is this what I think it is?" he asked, leaning forward to savor the smell of the meat.

"Yep," said Mary. "Saddle of elk in morel and juniper berry sauce. Plus local wild rice, marinated Brussels sprouts, and white truffle mashed potatoes."

"You spoil me."

Mary slid into her chair. "I had to. I felt guilty. I know what this night means to you and Annabelle."

"How could you possibly know that?"

"She called this afternoon. Asked me to do something special for you, with her love. I sure hope you appreciate that wife of yours."

"Oh, I do," said Dan. "I do."

It was a pleasant dinner. Dan had always enjoyed the Masons. They reminded him of the Iowa wing of his family: good, reliable, happy people who worked hard, enjoyed a good laugh, and weren't impressed by all of the extravagance that surrounded them. Over dessert, a thoroughly stuffed Dan asked about the new Mrs. Validator. Mary frowned. "Breeding tells," she said. "And when you give your child a stripper name like Amber, you've got to know what you're going to get."

"That's pretty harsh," Dan said. "I take it that you're not a big fan."

"Figured that out, did you?" She forced a smile, but it looked more like a grimace. "Actually, it's not too bad. At first, when she was wandering around this big ol' house acting all air-fairy like she had just won the lottery..."

"Which she did," interjected Virgil.

"... she was a pain in the ass. I even thought about quitting. I mean, a week before he proposed she's—excuse my French—a fucking cocktail waitress with her big fake knockers being drooled over by drunks, and now she thinks she's the Duchess of Validator Ranch? That was too much for me."

"At least it was kinda funny," said Virgil.

Mary's grimace grew grimmer, "Washing your feet in the bidet and saying 'filay mig-non' doesn't make up for being a class A, gold-plated bitch."

"Wow," said Dan. "I've never heard you talk like this before."

"Never needed to. But truth be told, it's not so bad now. She settled down after awhile. Mostly, she was just scared. And now, she's got *ambition*—which is good for the rest of us because she's out of the house most days before lunch and not home until late evening. And when she is around, I just tell myself that she won't be around any longer than the other ones."

"Is she home now?"

Mary smiled conspiratorially. "I wouldn't be talking like this if she was. But you should see her soon. Don't worry about being sociable; she won't. I guarantee she'll clear out as fast as she can. She doesn't like Mr. Validator's guests because she's intimidated by them—and she'll intercom me to bring her dinner in her room."

As Dan was helping Mary and Virgil carry the dirty dishes into the kitchen, he turned a corner and nearly collided with Amber Validator. She was surprisingly petite, but as blonde and buxom as Cosmo liked them. She wore too much make-up. She was dressed in a fawn-colored buckskin suit that appeared to have been designed by some cowboy couturier, and she had spectacularly beautiful green eyes, now wide with surprise. "Oh! Hi," she said with a breathy voice as she backed up two steps.

"Hello," said Dan. He glanced down at his full hands and shrugged, hoping Amber would get the message that he couldn't shake hands. Did she shake hands? "I'm Dan Crowen. I'm the president of Cosmo's company."

"Oh… yes. I see. Are you here to see Cosmo? Because he's not here."

"Yes, I know. I've been told that I'm to see him in the morning when he gets back."

"Well, that's good. Have you been here before, er—?"

"Dan. And yes, I have. I was even here once when it was being built. Quite a construction project."

She nodded blankly. "Well, I just got in from a meeting and I need to… freshen up. I guess I'll see you in the morning." She started to leave, then caught herself. With a slight lift of the chin and an equally small drop in her voice, she carefully enunciated, "If there is anything that you need, my people are at your service."

"Thank you. And it was great to meet you, Mrs. Validator. I'll see you in the morning."

With that, Amber Validator spun around and headed down the long hallway to the master's quarters. Dan watched for a moment as she went, appreciating the view, then pushed any thoughts about the boss's wife out of his mind. As he walked into the kitchen, Virgil gave him a wink, and Mary, already rinsing plates, mouthed, "I told you."

V. 1.3

That night, Dan's dreams were filled with odd and unsettling images. Later, he couldn't remember any of them well, but only that he seemed to be in a perpetual, unresolved struggle: wild animals, sinister figures, giants, monsters, zombies, wraiths. Every time he was on the brink of escape or victory, or even death, he was snatched away and deposited in the next dream... only to repeat the cycle again. In each dream, he sensed that there was another force at work in the background — an enemy? the Devil? Just pure evil itself?—arraying these forces against him, laughing at his victimization, never letting him lose or win.

The night seemed endless, unrelenting. Every time Dan tried to escape into wakefulness, clawing his way up to consciousness, he found himself in yet another dreadful, unresolved dream.

He finally awoke, exhausted, to bright light streaming in through a gap in the curtains. With a groan, he rolled over and checked the clock. Nine o'clock. Jesus Christ. He dragged himself out of bed and stumbled into the shower.

Twenty minutes later, he made his way into the great room. The maid vacuuming the big Persian carpet looked up at him in surprise. So did her counterpart, who was using a feather duster on the bronzes. Dan glanced grimly out the giant window. The sun was high over the mountains, and the sky had already turned from pink to blue. He hurried his step.

He reached the kitchen, so friendly the night before, to find Mary busy at work with her assistant, preparing dinner. Her mouth was tight as she nodded to him. "I think he's still in the breakfast nook." Dan hurried on.

He found Cosmo sitting on one side of the nook, his long legs and cowboy boots splayed out into the passageway and a pair of greasy and empty plates and the dregs of a cup of coffee in front of him. His silver pompadour was longer and flatter than usual, and he was wearing a cowboy shirt and an old A-2 bomber jacket. He was reading through a stack of printed pages—no doubt a draft of his shareholders' address—and marking it with an automatic pencil, snapping off the lead and angrily clicking out a new length. When Dan reached the table, Cosmo tossed the speech down onto the plate and tossed the pencil after it. "You forget to set the alarm or something?"

"Yeah, I guess I did."

Cosmo gestured with a flick of his hand at the place across from him. "I don't have much time. Have Mary make you something to eat after I go. Better yet, have her make you something to take along. I assume you haven't packed yet?"

"No, but it'll just…"

Cosmo held up a hand. "Doesn't matter. I've got an appointment on the other side of the ranch. Some… property. The plane is going to take you back to the Valley as soon as you get to the airport. It'll come back for me. I'll go directly from San Jose to the shareholder's meeting. I won't have time for the usual meet and greet with employees. And I've got to take off right afterwards."

"Okay," said Dan. "A bit unusual. But okay."

Cosmo's mouth went tight. "We're just adjusting to your sleep-in, Dan."

Dan felt his face burning, something he hadn't experienced in years. "I understand."

"Yes. Well, what it means is that I was going to brief you on everything this morning over breakfast. Now, I'm just going to have to give you a quick summary. I'll have someone else—my new assistant—fly back with you and go over the details. She's already at the airport."

Dan nodded. He felt like a little boy about to be spanked.

Cosmo cleared the plates and cup out of the way with the back of his hand and held up his speech with the other. Then he dropped the speech back on the table and folded his hands on it as if in prayer. "I'm going to announce a major change in the organization of the company," he said. "I appreciate that you are CEO and, as you know, I've done my best not to interfere in the daily operations of the company since I appointed you to that position."

"That's true," said Dan. For an instant, he thought he was going to be fired. Now he realized it might be something worse than that.

"However, on this one occasion, I am going to exercise my authority as both chairman of the board and largest company shareholder to make a strategic shift. I know this is an unusual move on my part. But I'm also sure you'll appreciate that in all your years with this company I have never once interfered with your operations or second-guessed your judgment."

"True."

"And I am only doing so now because I have a strong sense, based upon my years of experience, that this is a move that must be taken right now— even if the positive results may take years to appear."

Uh-oh, Dan thought. *Years?*

"I'll go one step further. I am going to predict that you will not agree with this decision. Frankly, I don't think industry analysts, our shareholders, or the media will agree with it either. But that only makes me more certain than ever. You know I've taken risks like this in the past… and they've always paid off handsomely for the company. You know this as well as I do, since my hiring you was just such a gut decision. And I've never once regretted making it."

"Thank you," said Dan, but he wasn't smiling. "What exactly is this idea, Cosmo?"

Cosmo leaned forward and look Dan directly in the eye. "Validator Software is going to get rid of its sales force. You're going to replace it with outside, contracted sales."

Dan's mouth opened involuntarily. He didn't notice that he had gripped the table with both hands. "You're not serious. We've got the best sales team in the business. Why would we get rid of them? They—"

Cosmo raised a hand to silence him. "I know exactly what we have. I know all the arguments for keeping them. But I also know the reasons for getting rid of them—and my conclusion is that these second reasons trump the first."

Dan felt his stomach drop. "But I built that sales force—Tony D.—"

"They'll be fine," said Cosmo. "As you said, they're the best in the business. They'll be hired within a week. Tony D. quicker than that. And hell, we'll probably hire a bunch of them back as contractors."

"But why—?"

"I don't expect you to understand all my reasoning on this. I'm not sure I do. But Ms. Holmes will go over everything with you on the plane. I hope you'll be persuaded. But if not, I hope that you'll at least trust me on this one. I know that the standard response to this kind of change is to quit; but I sincerely hope you won't do that. You've done a brilliant job with this company. And if you continue to stay on, I think your best days at Validator are ahead of you. I don't want to lose you."

Dan slumped back in the booth. He felt wretched, like a man who has just been given notice of a fatal illness. "And if I decide I can't do this?"

"Then I'll be both saddened and disappointed. So will your people. And frankly, it would be an incredibly selfish thing for you to do. You may not like this change, but at least you'll be making it during good times, with your competitors reduced to pygmies. If you really care about your employees, you know that this move will have far less impact on company stock than it would have if you were to quit in a dispute with the chairman. That would crush the value of all of the optioned Validator stock your employees hold."

"Not to mention yours."

"No doubt. And my losses will, with the exception of a few institutional investors, be greater than anyone's. And yet I'm willing to lose all that because I believe I'll regain every bit of it back—and significantly more."

Easy for you to say, Dan thought. *Even in the worst case scenario you'd still be a billionaire.* "And in between?" he asked as calmly as possible.

Cosmo sat back and stared at the ceiling, then looked back down at Dan. "It'll be rough. A lot of people will see their nest eggs all but disappear. And they'll all blame you."

Dan looked beyond Validator and into the kitchen, where clean-up was underway. Everything else in the world still seemed normal; why was it only crazy here, in this little corner? "And if I decide not to accept that blame?"

"Your departure would be a great loss to the company," Cosmo said firmly. "And it would be very difficult to fill your position with someone with your ability. And, of course, no one besides me has your understanding of company operations. But, that said, everyone is replaceable." He smiled knowingly. "Even the founder. And rest assured, whoever the CEO of Validator Software is, they're going to execute the new strategy."

"No doubt."

"So the only question is whether that strategy will be executed well, with minimum damage to the company."

"You mean the company, with the exception of its sales force," Dan said. "Because they are on the street tomorrow."

"Yes, but let's say a month from now. And as I said, they won't be on that street for long."

Dan rubbed his mouth. It was if last night's dream sequences had never ended. "So that's it. You hand me a *fait accompli,* and I have to take it or leave it."

"Yes. Please give Ms. Holmes a fair hearing on the flight back. If I see you at the shareholders meeting, I'll take that as a sign you're staying. If I don't see you, I already have a statement prepared."

"I'm not surprised." Dan shook his head—and didn't try to hide it. *Motherfucker. It's already completely planned.* After one last glare at the preternaturally confident man across the table, Dan began to slide out of the booth. "I guess that's it."

"Yes," said Cosmo, unmoving. "And Dan?"

Crowen paused, one leg out of the booth. "Yeah?"

"If you choose to stay, you know you have to own this new strategy. It has to be your idea. Your project. You are the CEO."

"Thanks for reminding me." Dan got to his feet. "For a moment there, I almost forgot."

He didn't shake Cosmo's hand, and he didn't look back as he walked away.

V. 1.4

I t was an endless drive back to the airport. Virgil Mason hadn't even been in the house, but it was clear to Dan that he already knew the subject of the conversation in the breakfast nook. They drove along in silence, Virgil staring straight ahead through the windshield, Dan resting his chin in his hand and watching the countryside pass on his right.

Virgil was obviously not going to be the first to speak, so Dan finally said, "How's the hunting look this year?"

"Good," said Mason. "They're predicting a late snow, and this summer's drought means the big bucks will be coming down from the high country early looking for food. They're saying a lot of white tail and mulies. Haven't heard any predictions yet about elk."

Dan didn't know what else to say, but the conversation offered a welcome respite from the debate going on in his head. "Ever thought of hunting in Africa?" he asked.

"Oh, hell yeah. I'd love to. But that takes a fair amount of coin. More'n I got."

"What would you hunt if you could?"

"Well, lemme think. I guess maybe one of those curly-horned kudu. And a cape buffalo—though I expect Mary might object to me doing that. Too dangerous. Oh yeah, and I like to get me one of those black sables. They're something else."

"I thought sables were like weasels. Or minks."

"Wrong kind," said Virgil. "These are like horses, with big old curving horns."

"Huh. Never knew that. So no Africa."

"Not anytime soon, that's for sure. But you know, they got these ranches in Africa that have a lot of African antelope on them. I may just drive down there one of these days."

"Well," said Dan, "I'm not a hunter, but I may just join you. Sounds like a good time."

Virgil glanced over at his passenger and then back at the road. "It was that that bad, huh? I'm sorry, Dan. That's tough."

"Bad? Yeah. But tough? No. Surprisingly easy. Too damn easy. All I have to do is go along."

The jet was waiting on the runway, where they'd left it the day before. The powered chain link gate squealed open and the truck started out on the tarmac. As if on cue, the attendant appeared at the plane's door. She nodded as if clicking off a mental checklist, then disappeared back inside. By the time Dan climbed out onto the runway, the jet's rotors were already turning.

"Take care," said Dan, reaching out to shake Virgil's hand. "I don't know how long it'll be before I get back here. Give my love to Mary."

"I will," he said. "And good luck to you, Dan. I know you'll do the right thing. You always do."

I wish, thought Dan as he climbed the steps.

"Welcome, Mr. Crowen," said the attendant, looking as beautiful and fresh as always. This time her demeanor was more irritating than thrilling. "I understand from Mrs. Mason," she said, "that you didn't have any breakfast. So I took the liberty of preparing some coffee, bagels, and fruit. I'll serve it after we take off."

"Thank you."

"And," said the attendant, making a gesture with her arm like a model presenting this year's new car, "I don't believe you've met Ms. Lisa Holmes." She stepped back to reveal a young woman sitting at a table covered with documents. The woman looked up and with a slight arch of her eyebrows, offered him a small smile. She was very slim, with short blonde hair tucked behind her ears. Not quite beautiful, she was striking, with a straight nose and a jaw line so sharp that it might have been cut with a laser. Overall, she looked young, smart, and formidable.

Just great, Dan thought, an intellectual joust. What I really need right now is time to think.

But to his relief and surprise, Ms. Holmes focused more on the paperwork in front of her than on her fellow traveler. In fact, for the first hour of the flight, other than a little small talk about the weather beneath them and their favorite type of bagel—she liked sesame, he poppy seed—Holmes left him largely alone.

In the end, it was Dan, weary and anxious from waiting for the other shoe to finally drop, who spoke first. "Aren't you supposed to be convincing me to accept Cosmo's plan?"

Lisa Holmes looked up from her papers. "I assume that you've already made your decision, Mr. Crowen. If you've decided to go along with the plan, I'm here to brief you on its planned execution—so you can speak thoughtfully about it with the shareholders and the media this afternoon." She looked at him with steady, unblinking eyes. After a few seconds, she went back to her papers.

Dan turned and looked out the window. They had crossed the Great Basin and, as near as he could tell, they were just crossing the corner of Oregon. There: there was Crater Lake below them, with Mt. Shasta looming just ahead. Dan knew that he'd made up his mind moments after Validator dropped the bomb on him. The decision wasn't the problem—that would follow logically from the premises and an interlinking chain of consequences. It was the premises themselves that caused the problems. That's where the misjudgements were made. The prejudices. The compromises to honor and ethics. Long before he had left the ranch, Dan had already made his decision. He just hadn't yet figured out how to make it without despising himself.

It was as they passed over the great summit of Shasta, which rose with a two-mile-high white finger pointing up at him, that Dan turned back from the window to the young woman. "We had better begin," he said flatly, "before we run out of time."

V. 1.5

Back in his office, Dan tried and failed to call both his wife (who was at her Junior League fashion show luncheon and had turned off her cell phone) and Tony D. (who was playing in the annual Validator sales force golf tournament and had done the same). Three hours later, he found himself sitting in the first row of the annual shareholders' meeting. As usual, Cosmo had arrived late, and they'd had no time to speak to each other. Dan absently joined the general applause as Cosmo took the podium.

As Validator took the applause from the happy shareholders—all of them pleased with the success of the company's stock over the previous months—he looked down and swept his eyes across the first row. When he spotted Dan, his eyes stopped. No expression. No tiny smile of satisfaction. Not even a brief nod. Just a brief glance—and then the eyes moved on, measuring the accolade.

It was a standard Cosmo Validator speech—equal parts wit, hard data, bullshit, bravado, and unaffected warmth for all of the people who had taken a stake in his dream. If Dan hadn't known Cosmo better, he might even have convinced himself that the old legend had somehow changed his mind and abandoned the new plan. But he had no illusions: he'd seen Validator act like it was just one more day of many... until the very second he fired an employee or informed wife number three that he wanted a divorce.

And so Dan waited. His chair, though well-padded, seemed to grind into his shoulders, the small of his back, and the backs of his knees. He stared at a small light patch on the carpet where a square had been replaced. He assumed that anyone who looked at him would merely see the CEO, deep in concentration about the future of the company. And, of course, they would be right.

He felt the butterflies rising in his stomach. It was not a new sensation. How many times had he felt just like this before a speech or announcement? A thousand? Was this time really that different? It's supposed to be, he told himself, but after all the years, and all the compromises, victories and defeats he'd survived, what was one more—however it turned out? All that was really left to him was a kind of fatalism: to see it through, make the best of the situation, and deal with the consequences. Luckily, he had become very good at dealing with consequences—whoever named it 'chief executive officer' obviously had never held the job.

A slight shift in Cosmo's tone snapped Dan out of his reverie. He glanced up at the screen. It showed revenue and earning projections for the next quarter. Here we go.

"As you can see, folks," Cosmo told the audience, "while our business remains strong, the overall industry is undergoing a structural transformation. Margins will soon be squeezed from both directions—from our big but fading competitors who will have to cut prices to remain competitive, and by a new generation of competitors who will pursue alternative channels such as the Internet to pursue our customers…"

Dan tried not to frown or smile; it all sounded so reasonable.

"…for that reason, after extensive consideration, Dan Crowen and I have concluded that this company must move away from our current business model of discrete packaging and pricing sold by a field sales force towards a new 'web services' model in which our product family will be leased by customers and delivered through the Web. To that end, Dan and I have determined that we will be eliminating our sales force over the next two quarters…"

There was an audible rumble in the audience. Cosmo raised a hand. "I understand your concern, ladies and gentlemen, but this decision is the product of months of research and debate. It has been ratified at the very top of this company. I personally asked Dan—and thank you, Dan," he smiled and nodded towards Dan but made no attempt to catch his eye—"if *I* could make this announcement so that you can see that I am one hundred percent behind this plan."

Cosmo paused. His voice dropped to his best intimate tone. "Folks, I've always done my best to take care of… *our*… investment in Validator Software. And I intend to keep doing so as long as I'm still standing.

"There's a new world emerging, folks, and we have to be prepared to meet it. And that is going to require some changes. You've just seen the first of them. So please, be patient. Bear with us. We've been through tough times before—far worse than this. The ride is going to get a bit bumpy over the next couple years, but I promise we'll come out the other side stronger, and more prosperous, than ever."

There was applause. At first it was nervous and tentative, but it slowly grew. Dan wanted desperately to turn around and both gauge the magnitude of the enthusiasm and see who still sat on their hands.

The opportunity came: He glanced up to see Cosmo smiling at him, gesturing for him to come up on stage. Dan literally leapt at the chance, bounding up the four steps in two strides and all but trotting over to the chairman. They shook hands, put on confident smiles and turned to face the shareholders, reporters, and photographers.

Even as he maintained his cheerful countenance, Dan surveyed the crowd. The small-scale shareholders, few of whom understood the implications of the announcement, were applauding wildly. The few institutional investors—there was Morgan Bank over there, next to Calpers—had already stopped their formal clapping and were now looking on with curiosity and talking amongst themselves.

Further back were the reporters. The print people and the bloggers were already typing on their laptops, talking into their cell phones, or collaring passing employees for quotes. The two TV teams—one from local television, the other from Fox Business—were busy filming B-roll of the two executives on stage as their two reporters scouted for stand-up interviews. The speed with which these reporters were racing about suggested that they too understood the magnitude of the story in their hands. So much for Dan's quiet prayer that the story would be missed, or at least buried on a busy news day.

With a feeling of dread, he finally lowered his eyes to the figures in the front row. His executive team was still seated, looking straight ahead. Their faces expressed a look that combined confusion, anger... and, increasingly, betrayal. None of them were looking at Validator; all of them were staring at Dan. He owned it now.

Cosmo turned, grinned, and shook Dan's hand one more time. Cameras flashed. Cosmo winked—the eye away from the audience—and said, "Good to see you, Dan. I'll be in touch." Then he was gone, trailing clouds of glory, shareholders, handlers, and reporters.

V. 1.6

Ten minutes later, Dan sat in his office. The door was closed, and Donna had been told to leave it that way. The telephone had already rung four times. There were twenty-eight new emails, which Dan ignored, along with a seemingly endless run of instant messages and tweets. He turned his back on the screen.

He heard Tony D. long before he saw him. He was surprised how quickly his VP of Sales had heard the news and driven in from the golf course. Maybe he'd heard it on the radio on the way. Well, Dan thought, better sooner than later. He composed himself.

"Donna, I don't give a fuck!" he heard Tony D. shout. "I'm going in there."

The door flung open. Tony D. burst in, still in his knit shirt and green slacks, his face red and twisted with anger. He didn't even pause to close the door behind him. He obviously didn't care who heard what he was going to say.

"Tony..."

"Fuck you, Dan. Just fuck you, you backstabbing son of a bitch." Tony jabbed a finger towards Dan's face. "Twelve years, you ratfucker. Twelve fuck-ing years of loyalty to you, and *this* is what I get. Fuck you. FUCK YOU. I made this company. I made *you*. And you fire my whole fucking team? You fire *me*?" He slammed his hand on Dan's desk. One of the Cross pens bounced out of its stand.

"I'm sorry, Tony."

"Fuck you, Dan. You lying piece of shit. You know what pisses me off most? You fucking *planned* this. It'd be chicken shit enough if you were some good Nazi following Validator's orders. But you fucking planned this with him. How long ago, Dan? How long?" Tony D.'s voice was vibrating with anger. "You shook my hand yesterday. You let me go out on stage and make promises to my people you knew I couldn't keep." Tony D.'s eyes suddenly lost their fire. "You hung me out to dry, Dan. Why would you do that to me?"

Dan rested his hands on his desk, palms up. "I didn't have any choice, Tony."

Tony D. stared at him, shaking his head slowly. "The fuck you didn't, Dan. You are the Chief *Executive* Officer of this company."

Dan's hands became fists. But he composed himself. "Yes, I am. And part of that job is making difficult decisions."

"Yeah," Tony snarled again. "I'm sure it's especially difficult to make decisions about the future of the sales force without once consulting your vice president of sales."

Dan didn't reply.

"So that's it, eh?" Tony slapped his hands on the desk, and pulled himself to his feet. "You know it won't work, don't you?"

"What won't?"

"Your new plan. Even if you manage to put a net services program in place—and nobody's pulled it off yet—it'll take you at least two years. And you're going to lay off your sales force *now?* Are you fucking crazy? What are you going to do for that year in between? Go door-to-door and sell the shit yourself?" Tony D. planted his hands and leaned over the desk until his face was just inches from Dan's.

"You're going to fail, Danny Boy, and everything you've accomplished with this company—not to mention your oh-so-perfect reputation is going to come crashing down on your head. And you know what, asshole? I'm going to be standing there, watching it happen, and laughing my fucking head off."

V. 2.0

Alison Prue sat back in her Breuer chair and tried to look as presidential as was possible with a blue stripe in her blonde hair and her knees as high as her chin. Why, she asked herself, did I ever go for this 'Icons of Design' look for the décor? Has anybody ever actually *sat* on the de Stijl chair?

They were in eTernity's Harvey Milk conference room, hard by the Emperor Norton game room, the Allen Ginsburg video-conferencing center. and the Owsley snack room. The walls in the Milk room—it sounds like a kindergarten, Prue thought, which isn't far from the truth sometimes—were painted matte black, as were the exposed pipes and ductwork above her. It all gets so very damn precious sometimes, she thought. We're trying too hard not to look like the real company that we've become.

In front of her on a forty-inch plasma display, Tipo—spiked hair, facial piercings, indeterminate gender—was discussing the re-design of eTernity's home page. Tipo tapped a key and up came Google. "The lesson that Google taught the industry," he said in an affected lilt, "is the sacredness of the home page. It must remain inviolate, pristine, untouched, and pure. It is comforting because it is predictable. It is your safe launch pad. It is, as the name suggests, *home.* The only changes we should make are purely decorative—like transforming the font on Arbor Day, or such like—never functional."

He clicked the key again to show a familiar but obsolete image. "ETernity's home page began with the same underlying philosophy, but…" He clicked again, and the once-simple image filled with images, boxes and text. "We have lost our way. Our home page has become precisely what we set out not to become."

Tipo folded his pale arms across his black t-shirt, which bore a white image of Arthur Rimbaud. He pursed his lips with frustration, then said, "What we need now is a return to our First Principles, the philosophy on which…"

He didn't have time to finish. In the doorway stood Armstrong Givens. Even after two years, Givens' gray temples, square jaw, and conservative suit and tie were still a shock in this company of trendy twenty-somethings. "The only gay person in a gay company," he had once described himself, and Alison ruefully knew it was true.

"It's on," said Givens, his normally languid Southern voice surprisingly sharp. "And you're not going to believe it."

The entire team jumped to its feet and trotted down the hallway, led by Givens and Prue. The Jerry Garcia room was already half-filled with eTernity employees. "I Tivo'd it," said Armstrong, leading Alison to a seat in the front, "but from what I saw, it's everything the bloggers have been saying."

The room was silent. Even when the image of Cosmo Validator resolved itself through a quick focus, there was none of the usual booing and catcalls. Alison glanced over at Armstrong, who raised his eyebrows.

On-screen, Validator completed the main part of his speech. "Okay," said Givens, "here it comes…"

Validator's slightly muffled on-screen voice announced, "And so it is for that reason…" The entire room leaned forward to hear every word.

Two minutes later, as the image of Dan Crowen stepping up to the podium to shake Validator's hand appeared on the screen, someone in the room shouted, "It's a lot harder than it looks, Cosmo!" There was nervous laughter. Someone else yelled, "Bring it on, Validator. This ain't your industry anymore." This time the laughter was more forced.

V. 2.1

A lison waited for the crowd, its members now muttering amongst themselves, to leave the room. On the screen, Validator and Crowen stood at the podium being photographed. Alison studied them with narrowed eyes. Then she turned to Givens, who sat beside her. He saw her look and said, "We've always wondered when. Now we know. Here they come."

Alison nodded. "Let's talk in my office," she said softly. She rose, straightened her vest, looked back at the remaining employees in the room, and smiled at them. "Nothing we didn't already know about," she told them reassuringly. Several of the employees smiled and nodded in reply.

Armstrong knew enough to close the office door behind him. Alison sat at her desk, beneath the big Diane Arbus poster, and stared up at him with curiosity. "You remember when you joined this firm that I told you I expected you to on take a second role besides product manager?"

"Daycare center director?" deadpanned Givens.

Not even a flicker of amusement crossed Alison's face. "You've been in this Valley longer than most of us have been alive. You know these men. So tell me, who's behind this unexpected move by Validator? Who are we fighting? Crowen?"

Armstrong put a finger to his lips. "I've known Dan for a long time. Since his banking days. And this certainly isn't his standard operating procedure. If he were to do something as radical as this, he'd roll it out carefully over two or three years. He'd probably be late, but he'd do it right. No, this smacks more of the Old Man. Cosmo doesn't just shoot the wounded, he shoots the people he *expects* will be wounded."

"But Crowen is CEO now," said Alison. "Validator's hardly around. Doesn't that suggest that this is Crowen's initiative?"

"Yes it does. And that's what's so puzzling. I don't get it yet. But we'll figure it out soon enough."

"It better be soon enough," said Alison. "This is a major move by Validator Software. And it's aimed directly at us. And we better be able to respond intelligently... and quickly."

"Understood," said Givens. "But look on the bright side, Alison. At least I got you out of one those dreary and pedantic Tipo presentations."

Alison gave a small smile and pulled a blue strand of hair behind her ear. "Yeah, there is that."

Givens was heading out the door when she called to him. "Oh, and Armstrong? Work your old Valley network and find out how Tony D. is feeling about all of this. I'll bet he isn't very happy right now."

Armstrong Givens nodded knowingly, and disappeared.

V. 2.2

D inner that night was at Delancey Street Restaurant, the dinner place run by rehabilitated ex-cons just off the Embarcadero, south of the Bay Bridge. It wasn't a great restaurant, but it was good enough. The concept was admirable, and most important, it was just a couple blocks from the eTernity offices.

Alison rushed in from the foggy San Francisco night to find Dale Corman, her live-in boyfriend, already seated and waiting. And fuming.

"I'm sorry," Alison said automatically.

"Not important," said Corman, rubbing his hand over his bearded chin as he always did when he was annoyed. "I've already ordered our dinners."

"What did you get for me?" Alison asked as gently as possible.

"Does it matter?" Corman asked. "It's not like you're a foodie or something."

"No," said Alison, "I guess not."

"I picked out some wine, too," said Corman. "It's appropriate for our entrees."

"Good. Thank you. How was your day?" asked Alison.

Dale shrugged, his long black hair falling down his cheeks and onto the shoulders of his black Gibson t-shirt. He was always irritated by this question about his day, though Alison asked it every night. "You don't think I work as hard as you do? Do you have any conception of how difficult it is to write a novel?"

"I didn't mean it that way, honey."

"No. No. Of course not. That's why it's always the first thing you ask me. I don't make you justify what you do all day. Do I?"

"No you don't."

"That's right. Sometimes I honestly think that just because you make all the money in this relationship that somehow you are morally superior to me." Corman's eyes flared at Alison, which only made him even more attractive in her eyes.

"You know that's not so," she said softly.

"You're damn right," said Corman with triumph. "We each have our roles. And I bring the higher qualities of art to our lives."

"Yes, you do," said Alison with the sexiest smile she could manage. She was ready to go back to the apartment with him right now.

A stocky waiter with a bent nose appeared beside them. He said in a gruff voice, "I see the lady has arrived. Shall I serve your dinner now?"

An hour later, they were standing in the Lucky 13 bar in the Castro, drinking Chimay and shouting over a Tom Waits song with a group of Corman's friends, all fellow writers. It struck Alison fleetingly that she had no real friends of her own—only workmates and employees, and she knew almost nothing about their personal lives. Instead, she was here, listening to Kevin, 300 pounds stuffed into a black leather coat, leaning on a carved sword cane and expounding on the plot of Robert Lennon's *Mailman*. Walter, a 6'3" beanpole in a plaid lumberjack's shirt, had claimed that whole sections of the book were "insufferably boring," and now Kevin was arguing that the book's *longeurs* were its best parts.

As usual, Alison listened, smiled, supported her boyfriend, and endured the affectionate condescension of the "real" artists with which she found herself night after night. But this evening—perhaps after the news of the day—she found herself both weary and impatient with Dale and his friends. The loud music and red lights made her head throb. Her lust at dinner was now long gone.

Finally, when she could take it no more, she squeezed Corman's arm and half-shouted into his ear. "Okay if we leave early tonight?"

Dale made a sour face. "Look, I'm having a good time with our friends here. And there's some things I need to talk with them about. Maybe you ought to just take off without me. I'll be home soon enough."

"Okay, but don't be too late, baby," Alison said. She fished through her purse, came up with a hundred dollar bill, and slipped it into Corman's hand. "Save enough for the cab home," she told him.

"I can handle my own business," he told her, rolling his eyes at his friends. "Don't wait up." He gave her a quick kiss and returned to his conversation.

But Alison, as always, did wait up, if only to make sure that Dale was safe. Finally, her eyes heavy, she undressed and put on one of her late father's old dress shirts, one he'd worn to IBM's Almaden Research laboratory back in the day. She left the curtains open and climbed into bed. As she reclined against the headboard with the blankets tucked under her chin, she looked out on the lights of the Financial District and thought. As always, she willed herself to begin with memories of good times with Dale... but as always, within minutes, her mind moved to the next set of challenges facing eTernity and how she would deal with them.

And it was with those oddly comforting thoughts of her company, her employees, and her own role as CEO, that Alison gently slipped into sleep.

V. 2.3

She awoke early to find Dale snoring beside her, his hair across his face, his clothes balled up on the bedroom floor. She made as much noise as possible while putting on her running clothes, half-hoping that he would wake up and pull her back into bed. When those efforts failed, she shrugged and made her way out the door and down the elevator to the street.

It was a beautiful morning, the great City just awakening. Alison smiled briefly at the old black man who was emerging from behind the cardboard barricade he created each night in a nearby alcove. The man, who never spoke or asked for money, nodded gravely at her.

Alison felt unusually charged this morning. Perhaps it was yesterday's news. It had begun by being so troubling, but by the time she had fallen asleep, it had begun to seem like an opportunity. She had left her cell phone in the apartment, and now she had an uncomplicated, uninterrupted hour or more to jog down the Embarcadero past the many piers—from the Ferry Building to Fisherman's Wharf, then all the way back—and to work through her company's response. A run, a challenge, and a beautiful morning: it was all she needed to be happy.

By the time she returned to the apartment, her face and pony-tailed hair slick and oily with sweat, the street was filled with cars. More than one besuited businessman sneaked a peek at the trim blonde in black running tights and Google publicity t-shirt as she paced back and forth on the sidewalk to cool down.

When she returned to the apartment, she found that Dale had managed to turn over on his stomach. Hoping that he still might awaken in time, she stripped down to her sports bra and panties and set about noisily making espresso and a bowl of granola, yogurt, and fruit. But it was to no avail. And it was only after checking to see if his breathing had softened at all that she glanced over at the cellphone she'd left on the nightstand… and saw that she had a message.

A lump formed in her throat. Phone calls this early in the morning were never good news. She grabbed the phone. Glancing down at Dale, she decided she'd rather take the news alone and went into the bathroom.

Before she hit the Play button, Alison checked the number. Menlo Park. Odd. Less worried now, she played the message.

It was the deep, sonorous voice of Arthur Bellflower, legendary venture capitalist and chairman and lead investor in eTernity. "Alison," his voice said, "I apologize for calling so early in the morning. I hope you are there and are awake. I need you to come down to my office immediately. Shall we say 9:30? I will leave a message at your office as well." She could hear other voices, the deep voices of older men, in the room with Bellflower.

She glanced at the clock. Eight fifteen. Shit. This was going to be close. As she turned on the shower, she made a return call to Bellflower's secretary at Manzanita Capital to confirm the meeting. Then she hurriedly stripped and jumped in.

Twenty-five minutes later she was dressed and driving her Prius out of the underground parking garage and out onto the street. The old bum, now sitting on an aging folding chair, nodded at her. Alison looked up at the skyway: it was gridlocked with commuters. It'll be better the other way, she told herself, at least until I get to Woodside. Then I'll start praying. Glancing around and checking in the rearview mirror, she tapped in the number for eTernity, then sneaked the phone up to her ear under her still wet hair. When her assistant David answered, she told him to clear her schedule for the rest of the day.

V. 2.4

Highway 280 was clearer than usual. It was a magnificent sight: the freeway and its cars poured down the long Valley, the great Crystal Springs reservoirs on their right. The dark blue-green hills rose above the water, thick fog pouring down them in a wave.

Alison was always thrilled with this view; it was one of her favorite in the world. She had driven this route many times over the years—to her old jobs at Apple and Google, to romantic weekends in Half Moon Bay, and—impossibly long ago—when she had arrived from Portland, Oregon in a VW Golf jammed with her possessions on the way to her first day at Stanford Business School.

But today she barely registered it. What mattered was the traffic ahead as she passed through the intersection with Highway 92. *Oh thank God,* she said to herself. *It's moving.* Twelve minutes later, as the familiar little clock tower read 9:23, Alison swung around the circle at the entrance to 3000 Sand Hill Road. She shot past the old Sun Deck restaurant, where she had celebrated the first big round of funding for eTernity, and then swung into a parking slot between an Aston Martin Vanquish and a vintage Mercedes convertible sedan.

The elegantly dressed receptionist gave Alison a warm smile. "They are waiting for you in the conference room, Ms. Prue," she said with an educated British accent. "The usual? Non-fat latte and a shortbread cookie?"

Alison paused in front of the conference room, pulled down the front of her suit jacket, tucked back her hair… and tugged open the big mahogany double doors.

Inside, there were a dozen men, all instantly familiar to her. They were standing in knots, drinking coffee and talking; when she arrived, they all quieted and turned. It took only an instant now for her to recognize them as representatives from all the venture capital firms, angels, and institutions who held equity positions in eTernity.

The fear that had been lurking in the back of her mind ever since she'd heard the phone message now surfaced: *I'm going to be fired.* Why else would they make this show of force? She swallowed hard and fought back tears. She had only a few seconds to make a case for keeping her job and her reputation.

At that instant, Arthur Bellflower stepped into Alison's field of view. He had thick, short-cut gray hair, a tanned face lined from too many windy days on Scottish links, an impeccably tailored suit (the joke was that he could still wear the same clothes as he did in college, but he never wore anything for more than a season), and impossibly white teeth.

"Ah," he said. "There she is. The Woman of the Hour." He kissed her on the cheek and stepped back. "I'm glad you could make it on such short notice…" His left hand swept the room.

"I'm sure you know everyone here."

Alison nodded warily. Why was Arthur being so cordial?

"Well," said Bellflower, "we know how busy you are these days, so we won't take much of your time. I've spoken with each of the gentlemen in this room. As you know, they represent more than sixty percent of the ownership of your company."

Alison nodded.

"We find ourselves in unanimous agreement that we have a brief window of opportunity, much of it created by the Validator Software announcement yesterday… you did see it, yes?"

Alison nodded again, then cleared her throat. "Yes."

"Yes, I was sure you did. Anyway, we have concluded that this is the moment for eTernity to begin the process of making its first public sale of stock. We'd like to go out within the next six months."

Sounds of assent filled the room. Alison glanced over and saw Ed Lessing of Mayfield Fund, cup and saucer in his hand, smiling and nodding at her. Alison turned back to Bellflower. "An IPO? Now? This was supposed to be a couple years away. When we were bigger. And the market was better."

"Yes," said Bellflower, rocking slightly on his heels. "That was before. Now, after yesterday, everything has changed. We think Validator Software has made a terrible strategic mistake, one that tilts the playing field in your favor. The market is going to like that. You're going to need a lot of capital to consolidate this advantage—the kind of money only public ownership can provide."

And, thought Alison sourly, it's the perfect moment for all of you to cash out with enough profit to cover all of your other bad investments over the last couple years.

Terry Bingham, the hot-shot head of Cisco's corporate venture fund, spoke up. "Frankly Alison, there's no indication that the stock market is going to get better anytime soon. This may be as good as it gets for a while."

Alison began to respond, then put up her hands. "I'm sorry," she said. "But I'm confused. I seem to remember that when we founded this company four years ago, you all assured me that any decision to move towards a liquidation event—be it an IPO or an acquisition—would be the result of extended deliberations between myself and my staff and all of you. And that this event would be set for at least a year out to spare the company all the chaos and dislocation this kind of event inevitably causes."

Arthur glanced at the other men, then smiled at Alison. "That's exactly what we're doing, Alison, *deliberating*. That's why we're all here. And that is why you were invited here. We have all of the time we need this morning to *deliberate* on this Initial Public Offering idea, and to come to some kind of agreement on how to proceed."

"I assume all of you are unanimous in your support of this IPO?"

Heads nodded. "That is correct," said Bellflower. "Unanimous. And you don't need to do any calculating to appreciate that this group represents more than sixty-two percent of the company's outstanding warrants."

"So," said Alison stiffly, "it's a *fait accompli*. Why am I here?"

Bellflower's face became stern. "Because, my dear, we haven't gone this far with you—we haven't put this much trust in you—to suddenly overrule your executive decisions. This will be *your* choice, Alison. We're merely here to help you make that decision and to present our case."

Alison, sensing an opening for at least a little control over her fate, folded her arms across her chest. "Assuming I do agree with you all," she began, "what's the hurry? Why not take the time to do this right?"

Bellflower chuckled. "Oh Alison, really? 'What's the hurry?' I never thought I'd hear those words from you, of all people. From the moment we first met, here in these very offices, I can't remember a day when you weren't urging me to move more quickly."

Alison couldn't help but smile at him.

The door behind her opened. "Ah," said Bellflower, "here's your coffee and biscuits, Alison." He stepped forward and took both of her hands.

"Come, young lady, let's have a seat. We'll drink some coffee, tell some war stories, and have a little talk. Then we'll come to some decisions." His hands were surprisingly soft and warm.

V. 2.5

With her head swimming with caffeine and the implications of her decision, Alison pulled the Prius onto the 280 on-ramp. The sun was bright in the blue sky, and the fog had retreated back over the hills. The freeway too was almost empty.

What do I do now? she asked herself. What do I tell my people? I've never managed an IPO before. Heck, I've never been *in* an IPO before.

All she knew about Going Public was what she had read, that it was a miserable experience that tore the company in two for months, as one management team took off on an exhausting global road show and another team stayed home and tried to run a fast-moving company with half the staff. Just as bad, the entire company would have to enter into a 'Quiet Period,' when any public statement, any unprecedented media coverage—good or bad—could anger the SEC, leading it to suspend the offering... with all of the damage to the company's reputation and value that this would entail.

She gripped the steering wheel at the thought. All the years of work, all the sacrifice—and to lose it all with one wrong word.

But don't forget, she told herself: Going Public is a *good* thing. It's what everyone dreams of, isn't it? The big cash out. Everybody gets rich; everybody gets rewarded for taking the risk of joining a start-up. Isn't that what Silicon Valley is all about?

Yes, but no one ever talks about the other side. The handing over ownership of the company to anyone with a few bucks to buy a share. The required financial reporting—and the very public media scrutiny that accompanies it. And worst of all, the change in the employees... and the change in *you*. We've been family; now we'll never be family again. People—like me—who right now are willing to die for eTernity will suddenly take their new fortunes and leave.

And who will replace them? Mere salary workers. The risk averse. The office politicians. The gold watch crowd...

The car's tires chattered against the lane markers, shocking Alison out of her thoughts. She over-reacted. The Prius swerved into the opposite lane, nearly hitting a passing panel truck. The truck diver pounded on the horn and waved a fist at her. She recovered control and made an apologetic wave.

She found herself panting, high with adrenalin. When it didn't diminish, she quickly searched for the nearest exit and took it. She only recognized where she was when she passed the big, distorted statue of Father Junipero Serra as she pulled into the parking lot of the rest stop. She had passed this place a thousand times, but had never found a reason to stop. Now she raced the car to the first parking slot she saw, braking so fast that the little Prius rocked on its shocks.

She was panting more quickly now, and was becoming more and more light-headed, until her vision began to blur at the edges. Oh God, she thought in a panic, not this. She had hyperventilated under stress all her life—before going on stage as a girl, in the run up to her first public speeches and her doctoral presentation, even once as she waited for a blind date to arrive—but it had been a long time. And she'd never suffered from this during her whole time with eTernity.

Now here it was again, like an old warning from her past. With her head bobbing and her chest hurting, she searched frantically in the car for a paper bag to breathe in. It had been years since she'd carried one for emergencies. She tore open the glove compartment—nothing. The door pockets? Her blouse? The terror was coming on now. What if she fainted and injured herself?

She spotted her purse in the passenger foot well, grabbed it, tore it open, and shoved her head into it. With her face pressed against wallet, hairbrush, tampons, and a tube of lipstick, she slowly regained her breath using the tried and true method of inhaling her own exhaled carbon dioxide.

After several minutes, her face was wet with her own breath. At last, she pulled her head out of the bag and sat back against the headrest, exhausted.

When finally she opened her eyes again, she caught a glimpse of herself in the rearview mirror. Her face and eyes were red, her wet hair plastered to her cheek by tears… and a loose eyebrow pencil had drawn a black line across the bridge of her nose.

If only my future shareholders could see me now, Alison thought ruefully.

Instinctively she reached for her cell phone to call home. Then she closed it again and tossed it on the passenger seat. He's probably still asleep, she told herself.

V. 3.0

The cockpit door opened and the pretty flight attendant emerged, carrying two empty coffee mugs. She was laughing and saying a few last words to the pilots. After three months of almost continuous travel, Dan Crowen now knew that her name was Andrea, that she had graduated from UC Irvine with a degree in communications, and that she lived with her fiancé in a townhouse in downtown San Jose.

Andrea set the mugs in the small sink in the galley and continued on to the cabin.

"Mr. Crowen," she said just as the roar of the engines changed key, "the captain has asked me to tell you that we will be landing at Farnborough in about fifteen minutes."

"Thank you," said Dan. He glanced over at Lisa Holmes and nodded. "Okay, here we go."

Lisa nodded and began to gather up the briefing materials splayed out in front of her on the folding table. She had been Dan's almost constant companion in his travels around the world over the previous twelve weeks, as he systematically visited every Validator Software plant, research facility, and sales office—not to mention all the company's major customers—around the globe. Cosmo Validator had given Dan unlimited use of the Bombardier—a surprising move that almost convinced Dan

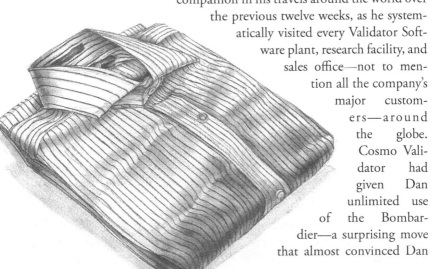

that Cosmo felt guilty—so they'd been spared the additional challenge of patching together a mix of first-class commercial tickets and charter flights.

But having access to a private jet had only made the marathon simpler, not easier. They'd been to twenty-five countries in ninety days, with Crowen rushing home at least one day each week to deal with the growing discontent at headquarters. Not surprisingly, Tony D. had walked out that afternoon and never returned, taking with him a severance package that most people could retire on.

Of course the company stock had dropped. Even a full-on Cosmo Validator charm session hadn't fooled the more cynical industry analysts. But the damage had been surprisingly small: within a week the share price had climbed almost back to where it had been before.

Unfortunately, it hadn't remained there. Dan had been afraid the announcement would set off a mutiny at Validator. He could have dealt with that. What happened instead was far worse. A kind of pernicious malaise had spread over the company as employees found themselves, for the first time, unsure whether management knew what it was doing, whether the new strategy would work, and whether Validator Software was still a winner. This last was the most dangerous of all, Dan knew. In the tech world, every industry had only a handful of "golden" people who migrated to winning companies, bringing their luster and consolidating that company's success.

As the dominant company in its industry, Validator Software had always enjoyed the presence of the best people in the field. Cosmo had drawn the first of them with his charisma and excitement, and Dan had kept them by giving them opportunity and recognition. The importance of wooing these vital few was the most important thing Cosmo had taught him during those early transition days.

One weekend, Cosmo had insisted on taking Dan duck hunting on Grizzly Island, just off the freeway between San Francisco and Sacramento. Dan had sat shivering in the blind, the Navy ghost fleet looming in the distance and the ducks mercifully thin on the Pacific Flyway as Cosmo—his custom Purdey at the ready—began to expound on how Silicon Valley really operated.

"I don't need to tell you how business works," Validator said. "Christ, you've been in the banking industry all your life. That's more cutthroat than anything we do in the Valley. You'll probably find us the image of sporting competition by comparison—shit, Danny boy, this Valley is more like a big frat house than a proper business community. The guys who started this town were all a bunch of wildcatters. They were best friends, they fought each other to the death, and they stole each other's women. Bless 'em. I knew them all, and my only regret is that I wasn't one of them."

Cosmo grinned. "Not that I didn't try. The fact is that not much has really changed. We're a whole lot bigger now, and a shitload richer, but scratch any industry in the Valley—including ours—and you'll find the same thing. We've all worked together at some time. Now we're enemies, but that doesn't mean we aren't still friends… or that we won't work together one day again."

He stopped, raised himself slightly from the bench to get a better view, and then sat back down. "Thought I saw something. Those damn ducks better show up pretty soon, or you and I are going to back to the lodge and drink cheap brandy.

"Anyway, that's the first thing you need to know. Silicon Valley, as big and famous as it is, is in fact just a small town. Everybody knows each other; shit, everyone's related to each other, at least in their resumés. You can be a fuck up, but if you belong in this small town, you'll eventually be forgiven. But if you're an outsider, you'll never really be trusted."

"So," Dan asked, "how do you get to be a local?"

"Stick around and start making connections. Nobody in the Valley is a native; not even the natives."

"How long does it take to get accepted?"

Cosmo shrugged. "Depends. All I'm saying is, don't be surprised when you don't get much respect from your peers—or even from the kid with the facial tattoos down at the latte joint."

"Got it," said Dan.

"No, you really don't," said Validator. "But you will. Now, there's one other thing."

"Yeah?"

"This town is the Pareto principle on steroids. No one likes to say it, but ninety-five percent of all the important things that happen in this town are done by five percent of the people. The Valley is about innovation, and innovation is done by geniuses, and everybody else is basically just standing around waiting to help make it work."

Dan scowled. "That's pretty harsh, Cosmo. You're dismissing an awful lot of people, including about twenty thousand people in your own company."

"*Our* company," said Validator, "and I'm doing nothing of the sort. That ninety-five percent is composed of good people—parents, Scoutmaster, soccer coaches, the kind of people you like to know. They're the people you swap Christmas cards with. I love those people. I'd die for those people— nearly have a couple times.

"On the other hand, those guys in the five percent, the geniuses—and they can be in the lab, marketing, sales, even accounting—are almost universally assholes. They know how good they are, and that usually makes them the most insufferable cocksuckers you've ever met."

Validator lowered the shotgun until the muzzle rested against the wall of the blind and leaned forward. "Now, here's the thing, Dan. The part of this job that will forever piss you off, and break your heart at the same time, is the fact that sometimes you're going to have to lay off some of the wonderful ninety-five percent. And at the same time you're going to have to do everything, including selling your soul to the Devil, to keep the assholes. That's because success follows them wherever they go—and they follow success in turn. Lose them and you lose everything. Understand?"

"Yes. But I don't like it. It's like Wall Street rainmakers. They're assholes too."

"Exactly. Except these guys aren't high rollers in expensive suits. They're just as likely to be represented by a bearded, autistic little fuck who will show you less respect than he does his pet tarantula—and who will never, ever appreciate what you've done for him. Or even thank you for it."

"Sounds awful."

Validator shrugged again. "That's why we make you rich. Now where are those fucking ducks?"

Customs in Britain, as always with the private jet, was brief and almost embarrassingly polite. An elegantly dressed young Indian man in aviator glasses was waiting in the lobby. That would be Ramesh, the driver. Beside him stood a disheveled middle-aged man with a comb-over wearing a badly-fitting suit. And that would be Arthur Hastings, the *Financial Times* senior technology editor.

And so goes the British Empire, Crowen thought to himself.

V. 3.1

Soon they were on the M40, heading up the grade through the white chalk cuts towards High Wycombe. Dan and Hastings were in the rear seat of the Jag Vanden Plas, and Lisa and Ramesh were in the front. So far the interview had gone well by Dan's lights, not least because Lisa had both her iPad on her lap and her notes on the seat beside her. She had chimed in with facts and figures to support any potentially controversial points Dan made—even handing back copies of the relevant article or report when Hastings proved skeptical.

So far, so good. But now the interview was taking a darker turn. Dan had known this was coming; he'd been through enough interviews to know the reporter's trick of starting friendly and easy, then coming through with the hardball stuff after you were softened up.

Now Hastings made the inevitable shift. "I'm curious—frankly, the entire business is curious—why you and Cosmo Validator would take such an extreme measure as letting go of your entire sales force to focus on a wholly new and unproven sales model." Hastings had dandruff on his shoulder and he stank of old cigarette smoke, but he was no fool; nobody got to his position without knowing his business. "Would you explain why you reached that decision?"

Dan had been asked this question a hundred times in the last few weeks, by employees and reporters, and by his own heart. He glanced back at Lisa, who was already digging out the McKinsey report that predicted a major shift to a web service sales model, even for complex and high-ticket product lines like Validator's. Then he embarked on his well-polished answer.

"Well, Arthur," he said, "one of the biggest errors a company can make is to stick too long to a practice that has worked for them in the past, and may even be working for them now, but is about to become obsolete. It's what Geoffrey Moore writes about: we're not just crossing the chasm, we're leaping over it… and we intend to be racing off on the far side before our competitors even realize they've been left behind."

Dan had said this so many times, he almost believed it. But this time it suddenly seemed fraudulent. Perhaps Hastings noticed this too, because he didn't write any notes.

"Yes," said Arthur. "You've been saying that for the last couple months. But I think that raises as many questions as it answers."

Dan felt his stomach drop. "How so?"

"Well," said the reporter, pulling on his droopy cheeks, "for example, what evidence do you have that this new model is the right one—or that it will even work? And, even assuming it *will* work, why would a company the size of Validator all but circumvent the transition process? Isn't it irresponsible to your shareholders to burn your bridges like this, leaving no escape path if it doesn't work? And what do you say to the claim made by some observers that this is nothing more than an overwrought response to eTernity going public?"

Dan froze, not from the fusillade of questions but because they so perfectly restated what he'd been asking himself.

Hasting took Crowen's silence for confusion. "I'm sorry," he said. "Would you like to address these questions one at a time?"

Before Dan could answer, Lisa turned halfway around in her seat, her knees tucked up onto the center console. "I think Dan was just waiting for me to answer your questions with actual data, Arthur. On the first question, as both Mr. Crowen and Mr. Validator have said on several occasions, we believe that time will prove us correct, and that eventually the world will see that we made the right decision. As for burning our bridges—hardly. I'd be happy to show you documentation that more than sixty percent of our sales staff has now been re-hired as contractors... and we can restore them as full-time employees at a moment's notice. As for eTernity, not only are the actions of a company one-fifth the size of Validator not something we worry about much, but I think if you'll check your own morgue, our announcement was made days before eTernity's IPO was filed."

"Okay," said Arthur Hastings, looking chastened.

"And finally," Lisa went on, "I have a report—which I negligently left on the plane—that I know Mr. Crowen wanted me to give to you. It shows, cost-benefits wise, that moving to a net app sales model is not a risky financial move, but is in fact the most conservative possible strategy. The entire report is proprietary, of course, but I'd be happy to share the executive summary with you. Would you like that?"

Arthur nodded, then turned. "Yes, of course, if that's all right with you, Mr. Crowen."

Dan smiled, "Of course. I'm not here to sell you, Arthur. My goal is to provide you with enough information for you to help your readers reach an informed conclusion about Validator Software and its future." He smiled towards Lisa. "Ms. Holmes, when do you think you can have that executive summary for Mr. Hastings?"

"Noon tomorrow at the latest," said Lisa. "You know all of the time zone problems between here and California."

"Will that be acceptable to you, Arthur? Or are you on a tighter deadline?"

"No, no," said Hastings. "That will be more than acceptable."

"Good." Dan gave Hastings his best benevolent executive smile. "Is there anything else you wanted to discuss, Arthur?" he asked. "Because we're almost there—I can see the 'dreaming spires' up there just ahead—and I don't want you to feel like I haven't answered every one of your questions."

Hastings smiled back. "Yes, that's about it. Just a few housekeeping questions. And we can do those via email if necessary. I don't want to keep you from your next appointment."

"That's very thoughtful of you, Arthur. It's always a relief to talk with a real professional."

V. 3.2

F ive hours later, Dan and Lisa were sitting in the Morse bar at the Randolph Hotel. The rest of the day hadn't gone any better. The staff at Validator's UK office in Oxford—sixty people, down from eighty-two just two weeks before—had appeared at first to be more receptive to the plan than their fellow employees in Grenoble and Versailles... but Dan soon realized that what he was seeing was merely the classic passive-aggressive British genius for appearing to agree with you even as they made you feel like a jumped-up incompetent turd from the Colonies.

By the end of the Q&A session, every member of the audience had his or her legs crossed and torsos half turned from Dan, who nevertheless tried to look collegial by sitting on the edge of a table with his sleeves rolled up. The final question, asked by an advertising manager in a chalk-striped vested suit—"Will our employee options ever resurface from their current submergence?"—so dripped with disdain that the young man might well as have just spit across the intervening distance.

This pleasant interlude was capped by dinner in the employee lunch room with the UK director, who obviously wanted to show his contempt for Crowen because he'd had to fire twenty-two sales people he'd personally hired when he was UK sales manager. On Dan's last visit six months before, they'd had dinner at Oxford's trendy Living Room restaurant, where they were joined by the Master of Christchurch College. Now the three of them sat in plastic chairs at a plastic table, and ate a ghastly steak-and-kidney pie washed down with some sour plonk. The director had an explanation for this rebuke, saying he had to deal with some "personnel problems." This, of course, was a less-than-subtle rebuke in itself.

The bartender brought them two brandies, and Dan and Lisa clicked glasses. "To a merry day in Merry Old England," Dan trenchantly toasted, then took a long slug. "Only Old Blighty can make me feel this bad."

Lisa slumped back into her upholstered chair. "Sweden tomorrow. Stockholm."

Dan shook his head. "Can't be any worse than today. At last I won't have to try to be witty."

"I thought you did just fine, considering," said Lisa, taking a drink and pursing her lips. "After all, they just saw one fourth of their staff disappear. You were never going to do better than a draw with these folks, and I think you got at least that. Once the stock comes back up, they'll forgive you, just like everyone else in the company."

"*If* the stock comes back up. The economy's already looking shaky. And let's not forget what's going to happen any day now: the eTernity IPO."

"Better sooner than later," said Lisa. "Get it over with."

"What do you think of those guys? Ever dealt with Alison Prue?"

"I only know what I read," Lisa replied. "Every new company looks great, because they're all about potential, not reality. ETernity's got good products, an okay business model, and a lot of talented young people… but it's a long way from there to being a proven success."

"Tell that to the stock market."

"I don't have to. The analysts are already doing that. But I'm not sure anyone is listening right now. Certainly not the small investors. They never do."

"How well do you think they'll do going out?"

"From what I hear, they'll do very well: $27, maybe $28 per share at opening. Probably settle there too, at the end of the day."

Dan whistled softly. "And us? What's the damage?"

"Down $2, maybe $4 by the end of the day. Then we'll get most of it back in the days that follow—once the reality of the challenge that eTernity faces, and Validator's built-in advantages, start to sink in."

"I guess I can live with that." Dan downed the rest of the brandy and ordered another. "Hey, I almost forgot. What was that report you were talking about in the car today with the FT guy? It saved my ass. How come I've never heard of it? It sounds like it could be really useful."

"It doesn't exist," said Lisa with a tiny smile. "I made it up on the spot. I'll write it on the plane in the morning."

"Jesus," said Dan, shaking his head. "You're good. That's about the third time you've saved me on this trip alone."

Lisa, finished her drink. "That's why I'm here," she said. "Cosmo thought you might need me."

"Cosmo was right."

"He usually is," said Lisa, signaling for another drink.

V. 3.3

Feeling no pain, Dan slowly made his way up the grand staircase of the Randolph Hotel, passed the Gothic revival stained glass windows, and eventually reached the second floor. Using his right hand to balance himself along the wall, he shuffled down the narrow hallway to his room, the Edwardian floorboards under the carpet squeaking with the weight of each step. He fumbled with the magnetic card for a while, but finally gained entry.

The bed was turned down, with a chocolate carefully placed on each pillow. Music was playing on the stereo. Most impressive of all, the curtains were open, revealing the vast, yellow floodlit Georgian face of the Ashmolean Museum across the street. The sheer romance of the scene was almost unbearable to Dan in his current state. *And here I am,* he thought woozily but with perfect clarity, *a lone businessman on the road. What a waste.*

He pulled off his suit jacket, then sat heavily on the bed, stripped off his tie and kicked off his shoes. He rubbed his face with his hands. Looking up, he saw that the screensaver on his laptop was glowing. With a groan he moved to the desk, sat before the device, and tapped the space key. The screen opened up to a list of new email. The clock widget in the corner of the screen said it was 3:00 p.m. in Silicon Valley. He never should have looked; now he'd have to answer the most important messages.

It took nearly an hour. Thank goodness he had empowered Donna to read his email, strip out all the spam, and send the non-critical messages to the right people. But that still left a score or more desperate emails waiting for Dan by the end of each day on the road. There were requests for interviews and speeches, introductions by friends to other people who wanted something, messages from the various companies and foundations for which he served as a board member, and personal notes from friends and family.

Growing sleepier by the minute, Dan tackled the business messages first. He answered most of them with no more than a sentence, deferring longer contact until he got home. He erased all the links to coverage by him in the media—Lisa got those too, and showed him all the important ones. He begged off most of the parties and gatherings, replying by cutting and pasting the same polite but pointed paragraph.

Finally, with his chin almost resting on his chest, Dan opened three emails he'd saved for last. All were from his wife. The first was tagged "Aidan." The other two were both empty, and tagged "Did you get my message?" and "Are you there?"

Too tired to feel any anxiety over the subject lines, Dan yawned and punched the key to open the first email:

———

Dan:

I hope you're doing okay. You sounded worn out when we talked yesterday. I know how difficult this has been for you. Having to sell a plan you don't believe in has got to be hard—and having to pretend you do believe in it must be doubly awful.

You've got that right, honey, Dan thought to himself.

So I really hate to bring this up, but I'm very concerned about Aidan. You've been so busy, I'm sure you haven't noticed, but I can't help thinking there's something wrong with her. Her grades have slumped—I checked with the school's grade site, and she's got an "F" in two classes right now.

As you know, she's hardly ever even gotten a C in all of her school years. And that's only part of it. I got one of those automated calls today saying that Aidan had an unexcused absence from her Geometry class. I called the office and told them she'd had a doctor's appointment—but I was lying. And when I hit her up about it last night, she told me her period had started and she was in the bathroom and late for class and didn't want to get hassled by her teacher, so she didn't go.

I knew she was lying. She cut class. And tonight she was talking a mile a minute, then she turned moody and emotional. I'm sure she did more than just cut school.

Oh, Dan, I'm so worried about her. And I feel so helpless. If I accuse her and I'm wrong, she'll never forgive me. But if I'm right, it could be even worse not to do something.

I know how busy you are, honey, but I could sure use your help on this. Is there any way you can come home earlier than you'd planned? And if not, can you call and talk to Aidan? I need to hear your opinion after you've had a chance to talk to her.

"No, I *can't* come home early," Dan said bitterly to the screen. "Do you have any idea what I'm dealing with?" I've got 32,000 lives, he thought—32,000 *families*—depending on me to get the company through this clusterfuck. They trust me. They depend on me. And I have to pretend like I know what I'm doing... and I *don't*. And all you've got on your plate are the problems of one single teenage girl—which probably aren't real anyway. Aidan's always been a good girl—and you're telling me you can't handle it?

He rubbed his face again. *Jesus, Annabelle, do I have to do everything? I thought we were in this together.* He believed himself misjudged and abandoned—and that was a satisfying feeling.

But neither the booze nor the anger was enough to cover Dan's gnawing sense that he was wrong. That it was always a mistake to question his wife's judgment. And worst of all, that he was being a poor husband and father.

He started to type a reply, but realized he didn't know what to say, and couldn't even formulate a proper sentence. He closed the laptop and dragged himself to bed.

V. 3.4

The Pacific Ocean was black and endless and almost indistinguishable from the sky, except for a few bright stars that burned their way through the scrim of the plane's thick windows. Sydney to Tokyo. Eleven hours—just two to go. Alison flicked on her overhead light and looked around.

Jenny Randall, eTernity's business development director and the only other woman on the road show, sat beside her, reading Jane Austen. "I figured this might be my only chance," she'd said when Alison had first noticed it. The six men on the trip—four from eTernity, two from the underwriter—were all camped out asleep in various states of discomfort. Alison could hear at least two of them snoring. And after ten days and 23,000 miles into the twelve-day trip, the chartered airplane cabin smelled of dirty clothes, sweat, and over-applied deodorant—hotel sinks and laundry services notwithstanding.

Alison knew she should be asleep too—she'd been up for twenty-two hours—but after the raucous, upbeat presentation in Australia, she was still pumped with adrenalin. *Can this IPO really happen?* she asked herself. More important now, could it really be as big as some analysts were predicting—$45 per share? Nobody in tech had seen that kind of launch since the crazy old days of the Dot.com bubble.

Over the last two months, she had formed her two management teams— one for eTernity under Armstrong, one for the road show; she had checked every fact and parsed every sentence of the company's prospectus, and helped put together the road show presentation materials. She had been so relentlessly focused that she'd scarcely had time to think about the ultimate goal itself.

And some of that had been intentional. ETernity would become a publicly traded company—with new reporting requirements, thousands of new shareholders, and the incredible wealth that was about to be dropped on her and her team. The implications were so great that Alison—as had always been her way—had put her head down and spent all her time making sure all the steps between now and then were done to the best of her ability.

But now it was real. The reaction at Sydney, and the growing excitement at each of the stops leading up to it, had proved that. More than, it was starting to look *better* than real: eTernity was not only going to go public in the new few days or weeks—depending on when the underwriter thought the market was ripe—but it also might go out in one of those supernova tech IPOs—like Apple, Netscape, Google—which had came to define its era. The company was going to be the latest phenom, the standard by which the next few years of tech company offerings would be defined. The media attention would be ten times what it was now... and so would the scrutiny.

And not least—oh God, not least—was the fact that everybody on this plane, and nearly every one of the people back at the office in San Francisco, was about to become immensely, insanely rich. She had tried not to do the calculations for her own potential wealth, but she couldn't help herself. Frightened, she had stopped counting at $175 million. *On paper*, she reminded herself. Between the employee lock-out period and the time it would take for all of the shares to vest, it would be twenty-four months before she'd be able to sell her thousands of shares of stock... if she wanted to. And why should she? Despite the impending arrival of legions of new owners, eTernity was still *her* company. From here on, every share she sold would be that much reduction in her power and influence over the company. Selling would be like cutting away her own flesh.

Alison glanced over at Jenny, who was still lost in her reading. What loyalty does *she* have in the company? she wondered. This company is my dream; what is her secret dream that sudden riches will finally make possible? How long will she stay when she doesn't have to stay any more? And what about everyone else? Everything changes now. *Everything.*

She looked out the window again, into the endless darkness. As she did, she spotted a solitary light below on the ocean. An island? A freighter? A cruise ship? Whatever it is, she thought, it's a sign of life.

Forty-five dollars per share. It took her breath away. She remembered those early meetings in Arthur's office when they were meeting with representatives from the underwriter—Dan Crowen's old bank, ironically—and how they had predicted $22 per share at the high end. These days they admitted to being conservative at twice that amount. Forty-five dollars. It was unbelievable. At that price, eTernity—a company with $120 million in sales—would have a market cap of $2 billion. It was a value the company had planned to reach in six more years or more.

It would be nice, Alison told herself, if this stratospheric valuation was the market's vote of confidence in eTernity's products and management. But she knew it was just as much a reaction to the sudden shift in Validator Software's fortunes—and to the fact that the once invulnerable giant had made an unforced error and opened the door to this plucky young start-up.

Why did they do it? she asked herself for the hundredth time. She was certain, despite any real evidence, that it hadn't been Dan Crowen's choice, no matter what the media said. No, this was Validator's decision. But why? Why cripple the company he had built from nothing with his bare hands? Had he grown old and senile and nihilistic? Was he determined to take down his own creation and destroy his legacy? *No,* she thought, *it can't be that.* Too many people over the years had made the mistake of betting on Validator being crazy.

He must have had a purpose for making this move, but for the life of her she couldn't figure out what it was—or how, now that the Validator sales force was gone, the company could recover in time. In less than five years, eTernity could catch it, maybe even pass it.

So maybe the answer was the simple one: Validator Software had just made a dumb business decision. Alison shook her head. What an unbelievable piece of good luck. *Wherever you are, Cosmo Validator, I thank you with all my heart.*

Enough thinking, she told herself, driving away the reverie. *The die is already cast. All you can do is make sure you play your part the best you can.* She pulled open her laptop—the blue flash of the screen almost startled her—and began to read her messages. One of the smartest things her team had done was to insist on the extra lease price of a jet with broadband Internet access. Needless to say, it had led to a fair amount of funny YouTube videos and creepy Japanese porn in the back of the plane, but it had also made them all much more productive. Even more important, it made them feel linked to the company back home.

Alison answered a few emails and messages. Nothing really important, other than a nice "go get 'em!" note from Arthur Bellflower and some Google Alerts filled with coverage about the eTernity IPO. Most were the same: speculation but no facts. *Good, good.* No one at the company had shot their mouth off and violated the SEC Quiet Period—thanks in no small part to a speech she'd given a month before. Employees still talked about it; few had ever heard so much menace and implied threat in her voice.

There were some Tweets calling for Alison's attention, but she stayed away from Twitter. Eight hours earlier, still giddy from the Sydney presentation, she had Tweeted twice about how well the event had gone. Literally within seconds, she had received an instant message from the underwriter's attorney telling her, in so many words, to shut up before the Feds read these things and suspended the IPO. Red-faced, Alison did exactly as she was told. Her worst nightmare now was that *she* would be the idiot who wrecked the deal. She swore to herself that she wouldn't send a Tweet, post a blog entry, or discuss the IPO with anyone outside of the players themselves until after Going Public day.

Instead, she pulled up Dale's Facebook page. She hadn't heard from him in a week, beyond a curt "Busy. Writing." two days ago. Alison had long since grown accustomed to the paradox that serious writers were poor correspondents. Dale always claimed that it was because "real" writers fretted endlessly over every word, while "civilians" could dash off a note without thinking twice. Since Dale was the only writer she'd ever known intimately, she had no reason to doubt him.

She stared at his best photo. He had sharp, unshaven cheekbones and almond-shaped blue eyes that peeked out from behind long brown hair. *Look at how gorgeous he is,* she thought. She remembered the day the photo had been taken. She had rented them a house at Sea Ranch for the week. They'd spent that day walking on the beach, and had eaten chowder and crab for dinner. Afterwards, in bed, she'd listened to Dale read a chapter from his unfinished novel, then the two of them had spent a long night of blissful lovemaking.

She scrolled down to look at the other familiar and comforting photos. Instead, she saw a new image, loaded within the last two days. It showed Dale sitting in their favorite bar, drunk and grinning, with his arms around two slutty-looking girls with too much make-up and too little clothing. Alison stared at the image for a long time. Then, realizing that Jenny was looking over her shoulder, she cleared the screen.

I wonder what time it is the States? She called up the time zone conversion widget on the laptop. It was 11:00 a.m. in San Francisco. She opened Skype and fished the head-set out of her briefcase. *He'll be up by now,* she told herself, *and if he isn't, well, he should be up.* She glanced over at Jenny, who had returned to her book, and tapped in the phone number.

It rang six times before Dale answered with a curt, "Yeah?"

"Hi, honey, it's me."

"I figured."

"Know where I am?"

"I'm guessing in a plane somewhere."

"Well, yeah. Over the Pacific—well, the Philippine Sea to be precise—about an hour out of Tokyo Narita."

Dale didn't say anything, as if he was waiting for her to say something more. Finally, he asked, "What's up? Why the call?"

"Oh, I just missed you. I wanted to see what you were up to."

"Checking up on me?"

"No, no, nothing like that. I've just been stuck on this plane or in some hotel conference room somewhere for the last week, and I wanted to imagine being home with you."

"Well, what do you think I'm doing? I'm writing. That's what I do, as I'm sure you've figured out by now."

"Don't be that way. I didn't think that if I called this early I'd interrupt your writing."

"Don't worry about it," he said. "What else is going on?"

"Just speeches and long plane flights. Have you read any of the news coverage?"

"No. Good?"

"Oh yes. Very good. And wow, you must be working hard."

"Yeah, I think I've had a real breakthrough on one of the plot turns."

"Oh, that's great. I'm so happy for you."

His voice seemed to brighten at her reaction. "Yeah, I've been working day and night."

"Well," said Alison, "not every night."

"Huh?"

"I saw your new Facebook photo."

Dale's voice grew dark and suspicious. "That? Nothing. I went out two nights ago with Davey—you know, the bassist?—and he showed up with a couple girls… you know, dykes. He took the photo as a joke."

Alison called up the image on her computer screen. "Those are pretty cute lesbians."

"More and more are like that these days. Is there a problem?"

"No, no problem."

"Do you think I would have posted that photo if there was something going on?"

"Of course not," said Alison.

"Good." Dale's voice was triumphant. "So, when are you getting home?"

"I'm back in the States in a couple days, but have to spend two more days after that in Seattle and L.A. Is that okay?"

"Yeah, well, there's a bit of a problem. I'm almost out of money."

"I left you over a thousand dollars, Dale."

"Yeah, but you know. I took some folks out to lunch. Dinner. It's been lonely here without you."

"That's very sweet."

"So, I was wondering if you could tell me where that extra ATM card of yours is, and the code number. I just need to take out maybe two hundred dollars to tide me over until you get home."

Now it was her turn to be silent. Finally, she said, "No, honey, that ATM card doesn't work anymore. That's why I put it away. But look: if you open my middle dresser drawer and look under the box that holds my pearls, you'll find six hundred dollars. Why don't you take half to make sure you're covered?"

"Are you sure it's there?" Dale sounded excited. She could hear him walking through the house.

"It's there. I put the money in the drawer just before I left."

"Alison, baby, I love you. You are a true patron of the arts. And just think about what we'll be able to do after your big event."

"Yes. Yes indeed."

She heard the dresser drawing opening. "Okay baby," said Dale. "I've got to get back to my writing. Have a safe trip."

"Thank you. Good luck with the writing. I love—" but the call had already ended. Alison carefully removed her headset, wrapped it in its cord, and returned it to her purse. Then she sat back in her seat and folded her arms across her breasts.

After a few minutes, she felt a hand brush her shoulder, and turned to find Jenny looking at her. Alison smiled wistfully and shrugged. "Boyfriends."

Jenny, who had been married twice, shook her head. "Alison, there are good men and there are bad ones. I saw that photo and I heard some of that call. And I've seen the way you've come to work some mornings. Are you really sure this guy is worth it?" Jenny glanced back at the men, making sure they were asleep, then continued. "With all that's coming, are you sure you trust this guy to own a piece of you?"

Alison looked at Jenny for a long time. Finally, in the rote tone she'd polished over the last week, she pronounced, "I'm afraid I'm not in a position to answer that question at this time. I'll get back to you."

Jenny chuckled softly and nodded. Then she reached up and turned off her light.

Alison looked out the window. The edge of the dark ocean was now outlined by a delicate pink and orange light, spread across the length of the horizon. As she watched, sleepiness began making her bones feel heavy. *Thank God our presentation isn't until tonight,* she thought as the light slowly grew to a band of brilliant gold. Beside her, Jenny had slowly slid over against the arm rest, her open mouth now puffing out a single strand of black hair with each breath.

Abruptly making up her mind, Alison sat up, tapped the space key on her laptop to reawaken it, and called up Dale's text address and began typing slowly.

Dale, I've done a lot of thinking. We're done. It's over. I want you moved out by the time I get home on Thursday. Good luck with your writing career—I'll be cheering from afar. Alison

---

She paused, her fingers poised over the keys. *Ah.*

P.S. Take all of the money in the dresser. And take the car and keys. I'll leave the signed title with the eTernity receptionist for you on Friday. Don't come up. A.

Alison reread the note three times, fixing it in her memory. Then she hit the SEND key.

Everything changes now. Everything.

V. 4.0

The black Lincoln Town Car pulled up to the entrance of Manzanita Capital. "Shall I wait, Ms. Prue?" the driver asked as Alison gathered up her coat and briefcase and opened the door.

"Um, no, Shamir," she told him. "This could take all morning, Maybe all day. Just be where I can call you if I need you."

"I will. And, Ms. Prue, good luck today." Shamir read the papers too.

She nodded at him. "It'll be luck. Because there's nothing left to do." As she climbed out, the sprinklers were still going, and the streetlights along Sand Hill Road were still on. In the distance, the rising sun was just beginning to illuminate the tops of the green hills of the Coast Range. Alison took a deep breath. *Remember this.*

Inside, the lobby of Manzanita Capital was still dark and deserted, but she could see brilliant yellow light and hear men's voices down the hall in the conference room. She was reminded of her last visit to that room, three months before. Then she'd been the target, the odd "man" out. Now—with luck—she was about to be the Belle of the Ball.

Most of the board of directors and representatives from the major investors were there, gathered in knots, shaking hands and chattering in excited voices. It was the same crowd as last time, but now they showed relaxed, happy, confident faces.

The room had also been transformed: plasma displays and television monitors had been set up on a pair of long tables against the far wall. Some tables held rolling Quotrons, others cable news; one held a live feed from Times Square with its camera aimed at the window of the NASDAQ display. Another table bore two large platters, one filled with sweet rolls, croissants, fresh fruit, and yogurt, the other covered with a sheet, and no doubt carrying sandwiches and other luncheon victuals. Throughout the room there were coffee urns, buckets of soft drinks on ice, and stacks of plates and coffee cups. Next to her, beside the door, was yet another small table, this one stacked with copies of the *San Jose Mercury-News*, *New York Times*, and the *Wall Street Journal*.

"Ah! There she is!" said a deep voice. It was Arthur Bellflower, wearing a vested suit with a red carnation in his lapel. "The Lady of the Hour!" Leaving his group, he raced over to her and kissed her on the cheek. "Are you ready, my dear?" he whispered in her ear. He put his arm around her shoulder and faced the crowd. "Gentlemen. It may be a long day—and with luck, we'll end it with one hell of a celebration. But now, before we're distracted by unfolding events, let us take a moment and recognize the extraordinary job done by this young lady and her team. They have shown remarkable skill, poise and—one might add—*endurance* over the last three months. Today, we are all about to become the... beneficiaries... of their good work. Let's show our appreciation."

There was hearty applause. The response was just as one might expect, Alison thought wryly, from wealthy men who were about to become even more wealthy, and to have *their* own brilliance validated.

"Thank you," she said to the crowd. "It's hard to believe this day has finally come. Let's hope for a strong market to float us up."

There was a chorus of "Hear Hear!" Arthur gave her shoulder another squeeze. "From your lips to God's ear," he said, smiling. The crowd laughed.

When the coffee urns were nearly empty twenty minutes later, one of the investors, Ramesh Vempala of Sequoia, announced, "Market's opening!" Cups and saucers were dropped on tables as the attendees rushed to the screens. The room went silent.

Alison made her way to one of the Quotrons, where she was flanked by Bellflower and Ed Lessing, both with their arms folded and their jaws set. These were the moments they lived for—the payoff, not just for their own efforts, but for the investors in their funds. Every successful IPO, like eTernity promised to be, made up for a half-dozen bad investments in failed or failing companies and camouflaged any number of smaller mistakes. A great IPO, which eTernity might be, all but guaranteed that the fund would turn a profit... and improved the odds that the next half-billion dollar fund would be fully subscribed.

"Here we go," said one of the men. Everyone leaned forward. The symbol ETY appeared on the screen and began to trail across. Behind it was the number *31 1/2.*

The room erupted into cheers. "Yes!" someone shouted, and more than one fist pumped into the air. Arthur Bellflower reached over and squeezed Alison's arm. He spoke into her ear over the cheering. "It's going to be... no, it already is... huge. Historic. You've just become a very famous and wealthy woman."

Alison never heard him. In her ears, the roar of the room had receded. There was only the screen and its unmistakable number. For her, its crawl across the screen had slowed almost to a halt. She found herself remembering being a little girl, driving with her parents on a vacation down the California coast just a year or two before their divorce and her father's fatal heart attack. They had driven down Highway 1 through Big Sur and along that wild, beautiful coast. They'd stayed the night at Highlands Inn, where her parents had spent their honeymoon years before.

In the morning, her father had promised Alison she was going to see something special, "a tycoon's home." She didn't know what a tycoon was, but she got the idea it was someone very, very rich. Like Scrooge McDuck. As they'd climbed out of the car in the parking lot of the visitor center, Alison's father had pointed up the hill to a pair of domed towers, beautiful and white in the distance, like the castle of a great king. "It's called San Simeon," he'd told her. "It's Hearst's Castle."

Suspended in time, the symbol and number finally completed its trek across the screen and disappeared. An instant later, it appeared again on the other side, moving smartly from right to left. But this time, the number that accompanied it was *32 1/8.* Someone in the crowd whistled his approval.

"I'm not sure my old heart can take this," said Arthur Bellflower. But he leaned closer towards the screen.

ETY had crossed the screen forty more times, its steady climb by eighths punctuated only by an occasional pause—never a loss—when it reached *37 7/8*. "I think we should sit down and have a good breakfast," said Bellflower, turning away. "It's going to be a long, draining day." In a daze, Alison followed him. *Rosebud*, she thought to herself, not knowing that she had just laughed out loud.

V. 4.1

I t was already evening in Heidelberg, and the rain and gloom were stripping even the picturesque old college town of its cheer. Dan had promised Annabelle that he'd buy Aidan a nice Christmas gift while he was in Germany—and this being his last day, he had carved out time for an expedition in Heidelberg's shopping district. He hadn't known at the time what a constructive choice this would be: it gave him a chance to clear his head after a spectacularly awful day.

The plan had been to fly down from Brussels to Mannheim at dawn, then spend the morning visiting the Validator plant just outside the city. After that, it would be lunch and couple hours of media interviews, then a car would drive Dan and Lisa to Heidelberg. Lisa had spent a year there as an undergraduate, and would visit a favorite old professor while Dan shopped. On her recommendation, they would then check in and grab some dinner at the Dueling House at the Hotel *die Hirschgasse*, then walk over the Rhine and up the hill to the great castle, where they'd enjoy its evocative lighting.

It had all looked good on the travel schedule, but even before they climbed on the jet in Brussels, Dan already knew that nothing was going to go as planned. Unlike the UK/Scandinavia/Russia trip a month before—or even the Far Eastern trip two weeks later—this trip was proving to be less a rallying of the troops, and more a triage tour. The chaos ignited by the announcement at the annual meeting had grown by the day, as complaints from customers increased in volume and anger. Now even the most loyal and patient twenty-year customers were angry—and were no doubt looking elsewhere.

He had seen the early numbers. Revenues had flattened. Margins had risen slightly, but not enough to justify the loss of an entire dedicated sales force. There were enough accounting tricks—held-over earnings, write-offs, late bookings—to put up a nice cosmetic financial front, but Dan had been around long enough to know that nobody would be fooled for long. The market and its analysts, reporters, and bloggers were all scrutinizing Validator Software's every move, ready to pounce on the first sign of weakness and declare the move a failure. He was secretly aware that the stock price was already softening. It hadn't fallen yet, but that was only because the booming stock market was still managing to lift all boats, even the leaking ones.

It was only a matter of time. The growth of Validator's stock, just four months ago the gold standard of the industry, was now falling well behind the competition—even the also-rans like CMR. No doubt the market was also factoring in the eTernity IPO, which could happen at any moment. But that was at the expected price of $26 per share. If it went much higher than that, the IPO could send another shock wave through the industry, and Validator would be in serious trouble.

But even assuming that eTernity's offering went as predicted, the entire electronics industry would wake up the next morning with the knowledge that there was a major new player on the scene. ETernity would have stolen industry leadership—and already some top talent—from one of the most storied companies in tech, and they would have a huge war chest of cash on hand to consolidate their new position. Now, when the time came for investors to make their next major capital purchase, where would they go? To the giant old company that seemed confused and lost, or to the hot young company that the world had designated as the next big thing? The answer was in the question, and Dan knew it.

So did everyone else at Validator Software. Now, as he raced around the world trying to buck up his demoralized troops, he found himself looking out over the sullen and dispirited crowds and asking himself: *How many of you already have your updated resumés on the street?* Was it the ones with the confrontational questions and the angry faces? Or the ones who turned away when he looked at their part of the room?

The visits to major customers were, if possible, even worse. Several major clients had cancelled meetings at the last moment, without even the courtesy of offering an explanation. Even the gracious customers had no hesitation about demanding that Dan provide a dedicated Validator employee to replace the attention they had received from the now-absent salesperson. One Texas manufacturer, who had first bought Validator 1.0 from the founder himself, hadn't even shaken Dan's hand before dropping his pronouncement. "I don't know what the fuck you and Cosmo are up to," he'd said, "but I've already informed my IT people that they better have a back up program ready to go in case you folks commit business suicide. Nothing personal, you understand," he'd added grudgingly, "but I've got a lot of customers, shareholders, and employees depending on me, and I ain't prepared to take your kind of risk."

That man was no fool, Dan reflected. Neither were his employees. They read the news; they knew the long odds against the success of this new strategy. All of them were experiencing first-hand the company's struggle to create a web-based sales program robust enough to handle the complex demands of a vast customer base—and to qualify, train, and get up to speed a small-army of contract sales people. They'd heard the complaints. They woke up every morning asking themselves if they'd been foolish enough to tie themselves to a doomed company, whether their stock options were worth the paper they were printed on, and—if worse came to worst—if they could find another job before the economy slumped again.

Dan asked himself the same question a dozen times each day—mostly on the long plane flights, when he had nothing to occupy himself but his own thoughts. The gnawing fear, the perpetual jetlag, and the stress of dealing daily with angry and unhappy people, was beginning to take its toll on him. Thanks to a diet of half-eaten meals, antacids, and painkillers, he had lost fifteen pounds. He couldn't remember his last uninterrupted night's sleep.

And home was no better than the road. He dreaded going back to the Valley. At the office, there was the silence among the employees whenever he passed, the new secrecy among his senior staff, the stares in the restaurants. At home, Aidan was sullen, resentful, and quick to shout. She had taken to wearing black and had gotten a tongue piercing and stud without her parent's permission—a subject of endless argument with her mother. Meanwhile—and not without reason—Annabelle had turned her suspicions about their daughter's secrets into an obsession that seemed to fill her every waking moment, making normal discourse almost impossible. Dan was almost relieved when he occasionally woke in the middle of the night: only then could he be alone, away from the looks and the whispers and the imminent prospect of more bad news.

It was during just such a late night reverie, as he sat in the moonlight on the living room sofa and stared out the big window at the lights of the Valley below, that Annabelle found him. Wrapped in a down comforter, she curled into a nearby chair and wove her gray-streaked hair into a loose ponytail.

"This isn't worth it, you know," she said.

He didn't reply.

"This was Cosmo's idea," she went on. "Although he doesn't seem to be taking any blame for it. You're getting it all. And it's going to kill you if it lasts much longer."

"I'm tougher than you think," Dan said shortly.

"Maybe, but not as tough as *you* think. Have you taken a good look at yourself in the mirror lately? You've aged five years in the last five weeks. How long do you think you can keep this up?"

"As long as I need to," he snapped. "That's my job as CEO. That's why they pay me so much money."

"We've got enough money to last us the rest of our lives. And what's money anyway if you have a heart attack or stroke and end up incapacitated... or dead?"

Dan snorted. "Now you're being dramatic."

"Am I?" she asked. "You and I know four men your age who've died from stress-related illness in the last two years."

Dan looked out the window at the palette of blues that the moonlight had created out of their garden. "Look, you know it's a lot more complicated than that, and I'm not going to indulge your fears by disputing you case by case."

"Fine," said Annabelle. "You just keep telling yourself that, if it makes you feel better. But tell me something: when exactly does all of this end? Because if you've been through hell in the last three months, so have Aiden and I. If anything, the situation is worse now than when you started. I haven't read anything, or heard anything from you, to be reassured that things are going to get any better for months—or even years. Are you really prepared to put our lives on hold for that long while you try to fix this mess?" she demanded. "Especially since there's no guarantee that you ever will?"

"I will."

"Or die trying?" she asked. "What happens when it's five years from now, Validator Software is in worse shape than ever, you've wrecked your health, and you've completely missed your daughter's last years at home with us?"

Dan was silent for a long time. When he spoke again his voice was slower and more measured. "I remember when you used to believe in me, Annabelle. I remember when you used to tell me I could accomplish anything."

She sighed. "Honey, I still believe in you, but after twenty-two years of marriage I also know how stubborn you are. You never give up. And you have an obsessive sense of responsibility..."

"And that's a bad thing?" Dan snapped.

Annabelle held her hand up. It was pale blue in the moonlight. "Let me finish. Those are things I love about you. They make you a remarkable man.

But you need to stop and get some perspective on all this before you plunge back into it again. You need to remember that you have *other* responsibilities just as important as Validator Software—responsibilities to your family. To yourself."

Dan gritted his teeth. "Do you really think for a single second that I've forgotten my family?"

"No." Annabelle put her face down into the comforter and seemed to be formulating her phrasing. "But I'm afraid you assume you can handle *both*. This isn't a normal situation, Dan. And frankly, I'm not sure you can handle *either* Validator *or* your family."

He reared up, dropping his blanket on the floor. "Great," he said sarcastically. "Thanks for the show of faith."

"Honey," she protested, "please don't take it that way. You have a remarkably analytical mind. And you have the confidence to believe you can solve any problem, no matter how big it is. But now you've got two problems, and I'm not sure that any amount of analysis can solve either of them."

He slumped back down in the sofa. "Okay," he acknowledged. "I understand you might think that my company is an intractable problem. I think you're wrong, but I can understand it. But I don't understand what you mean by a second problem."

"Good God, Dan!" she exclaimed. "This is what I've been trying to tell you for the last few months!" She stopped, and spoke slowly as if he were someone who didn't understand English. "Aidan. Is. Spinning. Out. of. Control," she said. "She's heading for trouble," she went on more normally, "and I don't know how to stop her."

"Oh please," he said wearily. "So she changes her look and gets a stupid piercing. Every teenaged kid in the world does that. I did. And I know you did a whole lot worse…"

"That's right. I did. Maybe that's why I can see where this is headed better than you."

"Or maybe you're just seeing more than what's really there."

"Is that what you actually think?" asked Annabelle, her voice raising. "You think I'm just some hysterical woman living out my own fears through my daughter?"

"No," he said hastily. "No. All I'm saying is that I make it a point when I'm home to spend as much time with Aidan as I can. I'm there with her at breakfast and most of the time at dinner. Yeah, she looks pretty silly. And she's developed a pretty shitty attitude. And she treats you like dirt. But I don't see anything you wouldn't find in half the homes in this Valley…"

"And half the homes in this town have kids on drugs or getting pregnant or committing crimes."

"Oh come on," he protested. "Even *you* don't really believe that. I don't see any symptoms of that in Aidan."

"Fine. So I'm over-reacting."

"Yes, maybe you are. I think you're just frightened by this crazy turn of events with me, and these unexpected changes in our little girl."

"And I think you're working very hard to ignore what's happening in front of your face!" She stared at him, then buried her face in the comforter. When she lifted it again, tears, metallic in the moonlight, were running down her face. "The truth is," she said in an agonized whisper, "that I'm afraid of losing both of you."

"You won't," Dan assured her.

Surely it isn't as bad as all that, he thought, sighing to himself as he got up from the sofa. He was so tired—and not a little resentful that his own wife had chosen not to support him in the single greatest challenge of his professional career. He knew he should walk over and hold her, reassure her. But he merely stroked her hair once as he passed by on his way to bed. Annabelle started to look up at Dan as he passed, but then turned away.

Back in Heidelberg, as he sat on the edge of a table in front of the nine employees who remained of what had been the Validator German sales office, Dan grimaced, remembering how he'd left that conversation. Well, as bad as *this* is, he told himself as he looked out on the sullen, resentful faces, it's better than being back in the Valley. *Really*, he thought wryly, *there's no place like home.*

V. 4.2

D an was nearly through his presentation—on the PowerPoint slide that he privately derided as the "kittens and unicorns" slide because it extrapolated sales and earnings out to an impossibly bright and sunny future—when he noticed that several people in the audience were staring at their iPhones and Blackberries and nudging the people beside them. Lisa, who was sitting in the back of the room, was also typing anxiously on her laptop. Dan felt his heart sink: here we go.

He opened the floor to questions. The first one, from a young man with flipped up Tintin hair, a manicured beard, and a disgusted smirk on his face, was the one Dan had been dreading for a long time: "*Herr* Crowen, it has just been announced that eTernity's stock has been listed on the NASDAQ exchange. Do you have any comment on that news?"

"It was expected," said Dan, trying to look calm and presidential. "Everyone in the world—including you, I'm sure—knew this day was coming. So, in that respect, it's good news. The speculation is over. No more fantasy. Now we can all get down to real-life business."

But he didn't believe a word he was saying. Nor, he suspected, did the young man, who had now folded his arms across his chest. And anyone in the room who did believe his words, Dan knew, was allowing wishful thinking to overcome cold logic.

There were only three more questions, all of them minor, and all searching more for comforting words than for any real facts. In the past, half the room would come up afterwards—employees would try to pass on private communications to the CEO, or suck up to him, or get their faces remembered by him, or just be able to say they'd met him. But this time, the tiny skeleton crew merely got up from their seats and shuffled out of the room. No one even thanked him for the trouble of flying halfway around the world to speak to them.

Dan was in fact relieved to be abandoned. He quickly yanked the projector cord out of his laptop and headed for the door. Lisa met him there with a stunned look on her face.

"How bad is it? Dan asked her. "What did they open at?"

"Pretty bad: $32, and they're still climbing."

Dan stopped in his tracks and looked down the long, empty hallway beyond the door. "Jesus. Anything else?"

"We opened down $5, but we're back up to down $3."

He chuckled ruefully, "So it's not an utter catastrophe, just a complete one. Come on, we have a dinner appointment."

But they weren't going to get away so quickly. Four reporters with photographers were waiting for them in the parking lot in front of the building. Dan grimaced at the sight and turned to Lisa. "You don't want to be in this camera shot," he said. "I'll go first and take their questions. You wait forty-five seconds, walk out right past us, and head for the car. I'll join you as soon as I can." He grabbed the handle of the door, and glanced back at Lisa. He winked at her. "Wish me luck. I get to be a movie star today."

The escape went as planned. Standing tall and looking confident, Dan waded into the small crowd as cameras rolled. "Gentlemen," he said, "how can I help you?" Four minutes later, as he began to walk away, the reporter from CNN was able to get in one final question: "Any message for Alison Prue and her people at eTernity?"

"Yes," said Dan. "I congratulate her on a job well done. And I welcome her to the ranks of CEOs of public companies. She's done a great job. I have tremendous admiration for her. But she's about to discover that this is a whole different job than the one she had when she woke up this morning."

With that, he turned and strode quickly to the waiting limousine, ignoring the shouted questions.

V. 4.3

D inner was destined to be distracted and moody, but the Dueling House did its best to make it appetizing. The many courses of rich food, the pretty face across from him, the engaging fellow diners, the extra bottles of wine, the old photographs of cruel Prussian faces with their fierce dueling scars—even the signature that a young Bismarck had carved into one of the table tops... it all conspired to build the most fragile of emotional bridges to keep Dan from falling into the deepest and darkest gorge imaginable.

After dinner they crossed a real bridge, this one over the Rhine, and went up the hill to the great castle. The cold and mist of the night made the landscape more romantic—especially to Dan, who was feeling the alcoholic buzz, the sensuousness of the proximity to tragedy, and the thrill, after so many years, of having a lovely young woman at his side as they strolled into an unknown and exotic locale.

Illuminated by powerful lights, the Heidelberg Castle loomed above. It was vast and the color of old teeth. And it boasted a mélange of eight hundred years of styles, from the medieval to the classical. It was less beautiful than powerful, a statement of brutal old civic power that no modern institution—be it a government or a great corporation—could match. "I'll bet those old Palatine princes didn't have to worry about shareholder meetings or the Securities and Exchange Commission," he said to Lisa. "They executed reporters and analysts who said bad things about them."

She laughed. "Probably. But you've got a much better retirement plan."

Dan was out of breath by the time they reached the top of the hill. By then, the mist had turned into a fine rain, and Lisa had tucked her arm in his. "Should we head back?" she asked.

"No. We've come this far. Now I've got to see this thing up close. We'll get under cover once we get up there."

They were both wet with rain before they found a covered walkway beside a closed restaurant on the back wall of the castle. From this vantage point, the entire interior of the vast castle was arrayed before them. To the left was a tall wall pierced by a score of classical, pedimented windows, all devoid of glass; and the upper two stories had no rooms behind them. To the right, an entire turreted tower, black as charcoal, had apparently been torn in two by an explosion and pitched forward to crash onto a grass-covered hillside. In the midst of this awesome display of Teutonic power, the fallen tower—the Powder Turret, which had been split by an explosion during the Thirty Years War—seemed a symbol of irredeemable weakness and decay.

Dan stared at the fallen edifice for a long time. "Maybe this wasn't such a good idea," he said.

"The rain's letting up," Lisa whispered. "Shall we go back?"

He nodded and looked away.

By the time they reached the hotel, his spirits had begun to return. Lisa agreed to a nightcap, and they each had a schnapps in the hotel lobby. As they touched their tube glasses, Dan offered a toast: "Now it begins."

A couple of drinks later, they walked up the stairs to the landing on their floor. "Where's it at now?" he asked, and Lisa pulled out her iPhone. "We're only down two."

"No, *them.*"

"ETernity closed at $37.50."

He took a deep breath and stared out over the stairwell. "That's a home run by any standard, isn't it?"

Lisa didn't reply.

"Well," he said, kissing her on the cheek, "good night. Two more days and we go home."

She forced a smile. "And we get to sleep in tomorrow."

Dan nodded and turned away, his shoulders slumped under his overcoat.

In his room, still in his overcoat, he sat slumped on the bed and stared at the floor. *How many nights lately have ended just like this?* he asked himself. *And this is the worst. I don't know how I'm going to get through tonight. I can't bear any more of this.*

He ran his hands through his still-wet hair. It seemed to him that the drops falling to the floor were from the rain, but slowly he realized he was crying. Ashamed of himself, he threw his head back, wiped his face with his hands, and sniffed back his running nose. *What are you, a child?* he asked himself. *A bit of bad news and you fall apart?*

Dan finally quit crying, but it was still hard to breathe. He felt an over-whelming desire to run away. But where could he go? He was already as far away from the source of his misery as he could be on Earth—and the fear was just as great here. Desperately, he looked around the room for some source of comfort. The TV would have the news. So would the radio. His phone? Oh, god no. The liquor bar? I'm drunk enough already, he told himself. His stomach felt sour.

His computer? He glanced at it, then recoiled. The news stories. The analysis. The blogs. And worst of all, the messages. Sympathetic, offering to help, secretly triumphant, asking for comments.

And Annabelle. There'd be a dozen emails from Annabelle. All sympathetic and falsely up-beat and telling him she believed in him, that they'd get through this like they had everything else. It was too much to stand...

Almost before he knew what he was doing, Dan was standing in his suit, wet shoes, and damp overcoat and knocking softly on Lisa's door.

The door partially opened and she peeked around its edge. He didn't say anything, but just stood in the hallway with his hair hanging down on his forehead and tears slicking his cheeks. Lisa didn't speak either, but her eyes darkened as she looked at his face and hair.

She stepped back and pulled the door open. She was wearing only a camisole and panties. Behind her, he could see the glow of a computer screen and an open ironing board. He sighed with relief as she reached out, took his hand, and gently drew him into the room.

V. 4.4

The Public House sports bar at the entrance to Pac Bell Park had been rented for the eTernity IPO celebration party. The cab dropped Alison off on the empty street out front, where she could see that the restaurant, tiny beneath the looming black bulk of the empty stadium, was jammed with her reveling fellow employees. She took a quick glance up at the bronze Willy Mays, then breathed deeply, steeling herself before she headed through the doors.

Linda from contracts administration saw her first. She was so excited to see Alison that she couldn't speak, but she did manage to hand her a t-shirt that read 'I was part of the eTernity IPO… and got a hell of a lot more than this t-shirt.'

It took a moment for the rest of crowd to notice Alison's arrival. As she took off her blazer and pulled the t-shirt over her silk blouse, she could hear the first rumbles of recognition. Then somebody shouted, "It's Alison!"— and all hell broke loose.

An hour later, she was sore and exhausted from hugging more than one hundred-fifty people, half of them drunk—including one woman who squeezed her a little too intimately—and all of them shouting their excitement and thanks into her ears. So far, she'd managed two sips from a margarita that Nguyen from accounting had managed to order for her, had been lifted off the floor and spun around in three hugs from large men she barely knew, and—in a moment the eTernity employees would talk about for years, if only to illustrate how much fun she *used* to be—had been lifted up onto the bar by two more male employees and asked to address the room.

Drunk and newly minted millionaires and near-millionaires proved to be an easy audience. Every sentence she spoke and every gesture she made drew cheers. Though she set out to say something memorable and even sincere, in the end she settled for the usual clichés: This is your big day. ETernity's success is yours, not mine. This is just the beginning. The best is yet to come. Etc.

The crowd's roar was undiminished with each drink and each sentence. Even in an alcoholic haze, everyone in the room—even those in their first job and too new to eTernity to benefit much from stock options—knew that this was probably the single most important day of their entire career, and they were intent on making it memorable and as protracted as possible. Sensing that their personal connection to Alison Prue might be important in years to come—if only as a cocktail party anecdote—they tried to hold onto her presence as long as possible.

Eventually, she managed to convince the men to help her down off the bar. As the crowd grew maudlin, one employee after another—many with faces slick with tears—embraced her again and swore their loyalty to the company and its long-term success. More than one employee, each thinking themselves original, said through sobs to Alison, "I'm with eTernity for eternity."

Finally she made her way back to the front door to retrieve her blazer from the still-starry eyed Linda. She backed out the door, saying her goodbyes to a half-dozen more people. Once out the door, Alison turned and started walking across the plaza towards the street, pulling on her blazer as she went.

"Boss!" shouted a familiar voice behind her. She turned to see Armstrong Givens, decked out in a shawl-collared tuxedo and silk scarf. She laughed and waited for him to catch up. They embraced, and Alison stepped back and looked her COO up and down. "Very dapper," she said. "I don't know how I missed you in that sea of t-shirts."

"I remained seated during the endless standing ovation."

"What?" she demanded with a smile. "You're not thrilled by all this?"

"More than you know, Alison," he said seriously. "This is, after all, my second IPO. I failed to sufficiently appreciate either the first one or its... rewards. Since God and NASDAQ have decided to bless me for a second time, I intend to drink this one to the last drop."

"We did it, Armstrong."

"Yes, we did. And not least because of our brilliant and talented CEO."

Alison blushed for the first time that day, and made a small curtsey. "Thank you. But I meant what I said. We all did this one together."

"Yes we did. And no doubt for the last time. I hope you understand that after today, everything changes."

She nodded. "Yes. I know."

"No you don't," said Givens. "Not really." He gestured towards the restaurant. "Nor do they."

"Do they all really believe what they're saying in there?"

"Pretty much. Yes."

"Should I believe them?"

"Oh heavens, *no.*"

Alison nodded. "Good night, Armstrong."

He kissed her on both cheeks. "Good night, miracle girl."

V. 5.0

A nnabelle was stirring bolognaise sauce in a pot on the stove. Dan stood in the kitchen doorway, bottle in one hand and corkscrew in the other. "Shall I uncork the wine?"

She didn't look up. "Fine."

He nodded, forced a smile in case his wife noticed, then turned and headed into the dining room. He pulled the cork, then took a quick swig out of the bottle. Not knowing what else to do, he sat down on the couch and stared hungrily at the *hors d'oeuvres* waiting in a tray before him on the coffee table. He thought about making a drink, but the bar was in the kitchen… and the last thing he wanted to do was go back in there.

No, he'd keep with the established program and wait for Annabelle to bring in his usual Bombay Sapphire martini with an olive in a frosty glass. The prospect of having her take this extra effort for his benefit—something he'd never noticed in the past—made him uneasy. He sensed that everything happening tonight was being tallied in a permanent emotional account somewhere.

Dan felt very alone—even abandoned. There was the strained relationship with his wife and the growing troubles with his daughter… and even Cosmo had sent him a message saying that he would not be attending the annual meeting tomorrow, and for Dan to host the meeting himself.

Has it really been a year already? he asked himself. Most of the annual meetings before it ran together in his mind, but he remembered last year's as vividly as if it had taken place a week ago. A year ago tonight he'd flown to Validator's ranch—and had missed this annual private dinner with Annabelle. Now he wished he could have swapped that night with this one.

He knew his wife felt that way, too. It wasn't just her anger; it was also her distrust of their daughter. Annabelle had kept Aidan under lock and key ever since she'd had been picked up by police in a public park near her high school in the company of a suspected drug dealer. There was no evidence she'd done anything illegal, but the cop had recognized the family name and drove Aiden home, rather than to the station. Aidan had denied everything, of course, and accused her mother of not trusting her, being a terrible mother, wishing her father was home because *he'd* believe her, etc.

To her credit, Annabelle hadn't bought any of it. She grounded Aidan indefinitely, even driving her to school in the morning, picking her up in the afternoon, and calling her at break-time and lunch. Aidan was furious and did her best to make life in the house a living hell. But Annabelle refused to break.

As relentless and steely calm as she was with her daughter, Annabelle conversely made no attempt to restrain her anger and resentment with Dan. The days when he was home from the road, the Crowen house was like an armed camp: Aidan slamming doors, screaming at her mother, and threatening all manner of self-destruction once she was set free; Annabelle answering her daughter through gritted teeth, then retreating to the kitchen or bedroom to bang dishes or cry; and Dan caught in the cross-fire, blamed by both sides, and plotting his escape with yet another business trip.

And now it was time again for the Validator annual meeting. There was no question that Dan would be home for it. There would obviously be no sales meeting this year. And as the event approached and he hadn't heard from Cosmo, Dan assumed he wouldn't be fired, either. But most of all, there was Annabelle's insistence that their annual dinner go on as planned, if only to maintain some continuity in their home life—despite Aidan's attempt to sabotage it.

But Annabelle seemed to realize too late that to have this dinner, she would have to let Aidan out of the house to spend the night with a friend… and Aidan made no secret that she planned to take full advantage of her temporary freedom. From the moment Aidan had left the house with a triumphant smirk on her face, Annabelle had been on edge… and obviously fighting to resist a desire to call every ten minutes to check up on her.

"Dinner will be ready in fifteen minutes," she said flatly as she appeared in the doorway, still in her apron, with a martini glass in each hand. "I'll have to go in a few minutes to put in the pasta. And I'll have to turn the meat then, too." She handed Dan his glass and pointedly took her own place on the far end of the couch.

He smiled wanly and reached out with his glass. "Another year, another annual meeting."

Reluctantly, she tapped her glass against his. "Let's hope it's your last... unless you've found you prefer life on the road with your young assistant." Taking a long sip, she sat back and stared at the far wall.

Dan looked at the same spot. "I don't think that kind of talk is called for, do you?"

"Only if I'm wrong," she replied. She turned to stare at him. Her eyes were puffy and her face drawn. "Am I wrong, Dan?"

"Of course you are," he said, still avoiding her eyes. He already hated himself for what he was about to say. "I can't believe you'd even make such an accusation. Especially tonight. I think you've been stuck alone with Aidan for so long that your imagination has run away with you."

"Okay," she said. "Let's pretend that's the real problem. Just exactly whose fault is it that I've been left here alone with our troubled daughter?"

Dan finally turned to look into her eyes. "Do you really want to go over this again?" he asked. "Do you think I don't understand my responsibility in all of this? Christ, Annabelle, you've reminded me of it every day I've been gone, in emails, texts, phone calls, and any other way you can think of to reach out and kick my ass. I haven't heard a friendly word from you in two months. Do you really think I haven't got the message?"

"Given your behavior, apparently not. I told you I needed you to be here. That I needed your help with this. And instead, you've betrayed me."

"I've done nothing of the sort," he said, stalling. "I warned you not to let Aidan get to you like this. It's affected your thinking. You're not yourself."

"And you *are?*" she demanded. "I told you Aidan was heading for trouble, and that we needed you here. And you didn't believe me."

"And I still say that you've over-reacted. I stood by you, of course. That's my job. But there's no proof that Aidan's been anything but a typical teenager testing her limits."

"Do you really believe that, Dan? Or is this how you rationalize the self-ish decisions you've been making lately?"

He put down his drink and leaned back on the couch, folding his arms. "Okay, fine. Do you really want to spend our special evening making accusations and fighting?"

Annabelle downed her martini and stood up. "All right. We'll just make believe that nothing has changed. I'll get dinner on."

V. 5.1

D an awoke, still dressed, in Aidan's bed. He didn't know how he'd gotten there—only that he had stopped counting after the third martini and that Annabelle had gone to bed crying. Having found their bedroom locked, he had managed to navigate his way to the nearest bedroom and fallen into the bed.

Now it was late morning, and his head was throbbing. He rolled over on his back and looked up at the posters and magazine clippings taped to the wall. The teen idols were slowly and inexorably being replaced by brooding actors, alternative rockers, and, most disturbingly, images of inked, pierced, and branded men and women from pages of tattoo and biker magazines. The images were so ugly at this time of the morning that he threw his right arm over his eyes and snoozed.

Eventually, the door opened and Annabelle shook him awake. "The office called," she said. "They need you in by eleven to do the walk-through of the meeting. That only gives you ninety minutes. I went ahead and cooked you breakfast. It's waiting on the kitchen counter, so you probably better eat it first before it gets cold. There's coffee too."

When Dan flung back his arm and squinted open his eyes, she added in a voice without emotion, "I'm leaving. I've got errands and a luncheon. Good luck today." And she was gone.

His hair was still damp when he passed Donna's desk, where she was talking on the phone. She said "Hang on a sec" to the receiver, punched the Hold button, and looked up at him. "Good morning. The latest draft of your speech is on your desk for your approval."

"Changes?"

"A few. There are some new estimates of market size. And they changed the earnings per share by two cents."

"Up or down?"

"'That's all they said."

"Then it's down. Tell them I'll be down in fifteen minutes."

He closed the office door and sat heavily at his desk. After rubbing his face for a few moments, he dug the bottle of ibuprofen out of the side drawer and tossed down two more to join the three he'd taken at the house. As the pain behind his eyeballs began to recede, he picked up the speech text and thumbed through it for the changes, all printed in red. The financial predictions had once again been downgraded—the third time in so many drafts.

It's never going to end, he told himself. This must be what it's like to slowly bleed to death. You keep assuming it'll stop eventually. But it doesn't. And though you try to stay on your feet, eventually you're on your knees. And then everything goes dark and you fall flat on your face.

He stood, pulled on his suit jacket, and folded the speech, putting it into his inside breast pocket. *But not yet,* he told himself. *For now, we're still standing.*

V. 5.2

I t wasn't until one of her new marketing directors stopped her in the hallway and asked if she'd watched the Validator annual meeting that Alison realized she'd forgotten all about it. She'd already read the analysts' predictions a few days before, and when the news came that Cosmo wouldn't be attending, she figured nothing important would be announced—and let the date drop from her mind.

It was only on rare occasions now that she even thought about her old competitor. Validator Software just didn't seem to matter that much anymore. Six months before, when eTernity was still trying to catch its giant competitor, tracking Validator's every move had been an obsession for both her and her team. But now that eTernity had stolen the industry momentum from Validator, Alison rarely felt the need to look back. All that mattered now was to consolidate those gains and keep moving.

"So, did you hear about the meeting?" asked the marketing exec. He was wearing a triumphant grin.

"No," she said. "Any important announcements?"

"None. In fact, the big story is that there were no important announcements. By the sounds of it, the shareholders were expecting something, *anything*, to restore their faith in the company. When Dan Crowen didn't give it to them, all hell broke loose." The marketing exec laughed. "I mean, seriously, there was almost a mutiny."

"Really?" Alison would have once shared the *schadenfreude* of hearing about one more piece of misfortune to fall on her competitor. But with her own first shareholder meeting just a few months away, she felt a twinge of sympathy for her counterpart. "How so?"

"Well," said Marketing Man, "people were audibly groaning during Crowen's presentation, watching him put up one downward revised number after another—and especially when he got to the end without offering a single solution other than what the company was doing already."

"That's because he doesn't know what to do. Cosmo put him in a box and there's no way out. All he can do is hold on and try to get the new system going before the company falls apart or he gets fired. He can't go back. All he can do is crawl forward."

"Yeah, well it sounds like the shareholders have begun to figure that out. Listen to this: You know he didn't want to do it, but Crowen threw the meeting open to questions from the audience, and this one woman gets up—a well-dressed, middle-aged lady; hell, she may have been an employee—well, she gets up and she asks Crowen what he's going to do about the falling Validator stock price. And get this: she's got a Blackberry in her hand, and she tells Crowen that since the stockholders' meeting started, Validator stock had fallen from 83 bucks to 81.25—and then she looks at her Blackberry and says, "And just since I started asking this question, the stock has fallen another 75 cents!""

"Oh my God," said Alison. "That's like a nightmare. What happened then?"

"Oh, the audience went nuts. They're like applauding this gal and cheering—and one guy started this chant, 'Sell! Sell! Sell!' until a bunch of other people joined in. Somebody caught the whole thing on his iPhone and now it's all over the Web."

Alison felt a shudder go down her back. "What happened then?"

"Oh, they got things under control pretty quick. But they forced Crowen to make some promises about the next couple quarters that are going to be almost impossible for him to keep. And if he doesn't, you gotta figure either Cosmo is going to cut his head off, or there's going to be some people camped outside Validator headquarters with torches, pitchforks, and a long length of rope."

The man chuckled at his image, and waited for Alison to do the same. But her face was set. "Then we better make sure we hit our own numbers, or one day they'll be waiting outside our place too." She turned on her heel and continued down the hall. The stunned man watched her go, then hurried on to tell his counterparts about the unexpected turn in his conversation with Alison Prue.

V. 5.3

Pierce Road was windier and narrower than Dan remembered. He hadn't been up here in years, since the early days at Validator when he was feeling well-off for the first time in his life. He'd briefly contemplated buying a vineyard up here, with a house at the ridgeline where he could look west towards the Pacific Ocean and east down onto the Bay by day, and where he could see the lights of Silicon Valley at night. He'd even convinced Annabelle to give her tentative approval—that was back in the days when she supported his every decision.

Luckily, at the last minute he'd recognized his own mistake. A winery? When would he have had time for that? In the years since, perhaps a dozen of his fellow Valley CEOs had followed through on the same dream—and lost fortunes on mediocre zinfandels and cabernets that nobody wanted. As his big BMW caught the narrow shoulder of a particularly narrow switchback and flung gravel a hundred feet down the nearly vertical hillside, Dan once again thanked his good fortune that he hadn't doomed himself—and doomed seemed the right word—to travel this road a thousand times in rain, ice, and the occasional snow.

Even after he'd decided instead to build their current home in a less dramatic, but much gentler, lane in Atherton, he'd still driven up here to get away from the intensity of Valley business life, and to look out over the steep green hills with their straight stitching of grape vines and dream of life after Validator. In his worst moments, he had gone up here to regain control over his emotions before putting his CEO persona back on and returning to work.

But that was long ago—when he was running one of the world's most admired companies. When his wife trusted his judgment—when he was worthy of that trust. And when his little girl still thought he was the most important person in the world, not just a jailer to be ignored, lied to, and bypassed on her headlong race down to disaster.

Here it is. Dan slowed as he rounded a familiar curve. There was a wide spot up ahead, where a tractor had long ago cleared away a small turn-out...

But the turn-out had become an entrance. Now, instead of rutted dirt and a low bank of gravel, there was a pair of brick pillars flanking a forbidding wrought-iron gate, each topped by a lantern. Beyond and below, he could see the tile roof, chimneys, and white railing of the widow's walk of a big new executive home.

Dan stopped his car with its nose almost touching the twisted bars of the gate. He stared in disbelief at the godawful new house, and the last of his emotional defenses collapsed. His company, his family, even his old dreams of running a winery, were all falling apart one by one. He let out a loud sob, and the tears began to pour down his cheeks. His hands were shaking so hard, he barely had time to yank on the hand brake and put the big car in gear before it rolled into the gate.

The sobs still came, one after another, until he was howling and punching the steering wheel and grabbing at his hair. He hadn't cried so hard since he was a boy, not even at his parents' funerals. Now it was as if every tear he'd ever fought back was rushing out in one great, paralyzing attack.

For a long while, he couldn't stop. His chest ached, as if a belt were being yanked ever-tighter around his torso. Finally he caught himself and rubbed his breastbone with his fist. *Am I going to have a heart attack now too? Is this where I die?* he asked himself in horror and shame. *Here, on some random hillside, after the most humiliating day of my life?*

No, he told himself as the tightness in his chest eased a little. *I won't be that lucky. God isn't that merciful.*

V. 5.4

The brief respite from tears had cruelly provoked Dan to remember the public humiliation that had driven him to hide in the hills in the first place. He'd heard the rumbles from the audience. But there was nothing he could do. Cosmo would've tackled the doubters head-on, challenging them to explain themselves, then improvising some strategy on the spot. It would have been mostly bullshit—but it would have turned the jeers to cheers, and he'd have worried later about actually fulfilling his promises.

But that was Cosmo. The shareholders, the market, and the public believed in Cosmo Validator because he had pulled off so many miracles in the past. Cosmo had that personality common to all great entrepreneurs: he would lie, cheat, and probably kill, to protect the company he had created. And the world knew that—so if he was caught fabricating numbers to buy himself time to save his company… well, everyone knew he was a rogue.

But that isn't me, Dan acknowledged to himself. He had lied and dissembled and tossed up so many smoke screens of false optimism over the last year that the prospect of ever doing it again made him sick to his stomach. It wasn't as if anyone had believed him anyway. He was a CEO, not a founder; a hired gun, not a true believer. That was why he had mercilessly cut all the bullshit financial predictions out of the annual report speech—and why, just minutes before leaving his office and heading down to the main hall, he had excised the entire last page of the speech. No more lies to the shareholders, he had decided; no more lies to the employees. Now we all live with the truth.

Some hero you are, he told himself now. *What did you think was going to happen? They were going to give you a standing ovation for honesty? Who were you kidding?* The real truth-teller was that woman with the Blackberry. She'd had it right: Say what you want, Crowen; be a liar or be an honest man— either way, it's just your own fucking vanity. All that counts is the bottom line… and you have failed.

Maybe so, he thought, but at least I don't have to lie anymore. Well… at least not about *this*.

He took a deep breath and wiped the tears off his face with his suit sleeve. Then for the first time, he looked around. It was beginning to get dark. Though the sky overhead was still blue, the sun was setting behind the hills, casting the Valley floor into shadow. Only the summits of the Diablo Mountains across the Bay were still glowing deep pink and orange. Below, the lights of Silicon Valley, from Burlingame to Gilroy, were just coming on. So were the skylights on the roof of the house before him, he saw with surprise. He hadn't given a thought to the possibility that there might be people inside.

Wouldn't it be awkward, he thought as he looked in the mirror, *if the owner's headlights were to show up behind my rear bumper right now? How would I explain this?*

As if on cue, Dan jumped as headlights flashed across the back window of the car. Then, to his relief, the car roared on up the road. He found himself laughing at his own over reaction. *What am I worrying about?* he asked himself. *The poor sonofabitch is probably like the rest of us: working fifteen hours a day to own a big house he never gets home to. He won't be home for hours.*

Well buddy, he thought as he flipped open his cell phone, *at least you've still got a home.* He googled the number for the San Jose Fairmont Hotel and called to make a reservation for the night. As he waited for confirmation, he looked down the hill to his left. He could still make out the white glow of the spiked tent of Shoreline Amphitheater and—further to the left—the even whiter salt stacks on the edge of the Bay near Redwood City. With his finger against the window, he traced the line of Willow Road as it came up the hill from Bayshore Freeway and the lights became further apart. *One of those is my house,* Dan told himself. *When will be the next time I see it?*

The reservations clerk came back on the line and confirmed his room. Dan thanked her, hung up, and tapped in a text message to Lisa: *Meet me at the Fairmont in San Jose in an hour. I'll order room service.* Without waiting for a reply, he started the car and backed out of his dead-end.

V. 5.5

When Armstrong Givens straightened his cuffs, Alison noticed for the first time that he wore a Cartier tank watch with an alligator strap. When did he get that? Had he always worn it, and was she just now noticing it? Or was this the first sign that he'd already begun spending his stock money?

It's odd, the things you notice at times like this, Alison thought. The first new cars had already begun appearing in the parking lot. Nothing too expensive, but that was probably because only the lower-level employees as yet had stock they could sell. Next week, the big shareholders would see their "founder" lock-outs end—and the first twenty percent vesting completed. And Alison had already been warned by Valley veterans—her new best friends—that the Porsches and Ferraris would soon follow.

"Hey," she told Armstrong before he had a chance to speak, "I was just reminded this morning that it was one year ago today—right here in Harvey Milk—that I first announced that we were going public."

"An historic moment," he replied. "Someday they'll put up a plaque outside." He had a weary look on his face.

Dreading what might be coming, Alison decided to keep talking. She gestured at the stacks of boxes and the empty walls. "Looks a little different these days, doesn't it?"

"Indeed," Armstrong said dryly.

"Are you going to miss this place?"

"You mean the vomit on the sidewalk out front? The ancient elevator with creaking cable and the zero-gravity descents? The lack of an edible breakfast within eight blocks? The disappearance of every parking space for a mile every time there's a Giants game? Oh, I don't think I'll ever stop weeping at the many memories."

"Well, I know that *I'll* never forget this place," she said, and tears welled up in her eyes.

Armstrong reached over and patted the back of her hand. "And that is perfectly understandable, my dear. After all, it was within these walls that you experienced something that only happens to one or two people per generation. I would think you would cherish this place."

"And now?"

"We're at the point of inflection, Alison, and you and I both know it. This is a very different company now than it was just a year ago. Eighty percent of the employees in the company today weren't here at the IPO. They have no memory of that plucky little start-up called eTernity—and they don't want to know about it. What they care about is the future of this company and their place in it. They know what this company is straining to be, and they're getting impatient about getting there."

"And what is that company, Armstrong?"

"You know that better than I do," he said. "It's the industry leader. A big, established, supremely competent global corporation with tens of thousands of employees and several billion in annual revenues."

Now it was her turn to take his hand. "And to think that you and I *did* this. Isn't it incredible? All from an idea sketched out on a paper napkin. A great worldwide company, employing thousands—an institution that will likely outlive us both. Doesn't that prospect excite you?"

He drew his hand away. "Not in the least, my dear. I loathe life in big companies. It's all about power and boundaries. And I've never been obsessed with the former, nor constrained by the latter. I know a lot of people for whom big company life, with all of its privileges and perquisites, represents a kind of empowerment. But for me, it's nothing but a slow suffocation. Big companies bore me to death."

Alison had unconsciously sensed this coming for weeks, but had refused to admit it to herself. Now the dreaded moment had arrived. She felt as if she were on the other side of the room, watching herself performing in a scene that would become an important—if largely inexplicable—part of the company's official history.

"What does that mean?" she asked.

"It means, darling, that inflections, transitions, *turning points*, are always the best times for arrivals and departures. And so I've decided to use this moment to make my own exit."

"You're leaving? Now?"

"No," Armstrong said, "not this moment. But soon. Within the year; as soon as my vesting is complete—and I hope you will speak to the board about accelerating it. Trust me, once you find my replacement, you'll want me out of here pretty fast."

"But I still don't understand why. You've been as important to making eTernity what it is today as anyone in the company. Why would you walk away before the job is done? Don't you care enough about this company—about *us*—to see this thing through? To make eTernity what it's destined to be?"

Armstrong refused to take the bait. "I *start* things, Alison, I almost never *finish* things—at least not if I can help it."

"But that's facile—it doesn't mean anything, Armstrong. After all we've been through, at least you can give me a sincere answer."

Givens was momentarily taken aback. Then he grinned at her. "Good for you," he said. "Okay, young lady, I'll tell you the truth. You're entering into a whole new phase in your career as CEO of this company. You're inexperienced enough in this job that you still believe that all the changes that are about to hit the company will take place around the edges. That the heart of eTernity, the one we created over the last few years, will always remain unchanged.

"What you don't understand is that *everything* is going to change around here. *You* are going to change. It's already begun in ways that you haven't even noticed yet."

She started to interrupt, but he held up his hand to stop her. "Don't try. Just trust that I know what I'm talking about. I've been here before. And I've learned two things. The first is that I don't like those changes when they happen to me, much less my company, because in my heart I'm an entrepreneur, not a businessman. The second is that this attitude of mine is exactly the wrong thing for a CEO at a time like this. What you need now, Alison, is a veteran Operations guy who knows how to help you navigate down the next stretch of road. Someone who wants to go where you're going. I'm not that man."

"And there's nothing I can say or do to keep you here?"

Armstrong gave a sad smile. "Nothing you say can make me the person you need now; and nothing you do can accomplish anything but insult me. Don't forget, you just made me a rich man, my dear. I can no longer be bought."

She nodded. "I assume you don't plan to compete with me, Armstrong."

"I'm too old for lawsuits," he said. "And besides, I'm going in a different direction now. I'm in love—and love always makes me hungry for good food."

They both laughed—longer and louder than they needed to.

V. 5.6

Alison was late for lunch at Lavanda. She had underestimated the time it would take to drive to Palo Alto, much less to find a parking place. She felt badly because she had asked for the lunch, and for Arthur to carve some time out of his busy day.

But Arthur Bellflower was still his jaunty, gracious self when she finally arrived, frazzled and embarrassed.

"How is my favorite businesswoman?" he asked as he rose to hug her.

"Embarassed, Arthur. I've been famously prompt my whole life. Now I can't seem to get anywhere on time."

He replaced the napkin on his lap. "You're running a public corporation now, Alison. You're going to have to learn a whole new set of time management skills and strategies."

She caught the waiter's eye, then turned back to him. "But I just don't understand. In the early days of the company, I had about fifteen different jobs, from making sales calls to hiring to cleaning the damn ladies' room. And, with a few exceptions, I was always able to stay on top of all of them.

Now, I've basically got one big job—and a growing army of people to help me—and yet all of a sudden I can't seem to get to a single appointment on time. I'm late for meetings, phone calls... and now even with you, my favorite person in the whole world."

Arthur was about to reply when the waiter suddenly appeared beside them. She could see from the look on his face that he recognized her from the burst of media coverage over the last few months. Alison ordered ice tea, and Arthur ordered his second gin and tonic. "I don't have to run a corporation this afternoon," he said with a grin.

After the waiter left, Bellflower became more serious. "There are two things you are going to have to learn very quickly," he said. "The first—and I'm not worried about this one, because you're a quick study—is that you need to develop techniques and find the right people and channels to learn what's *really* going on in your company. That's why kings had jesters, and we men have wives: someone has to be willing to tell us the truth."

She nodded. She was already dreading Armstrong Givens' departure. "And the second?"

"I personally think this one is even more important—though some may disagree. It is that you need to carve time out of your daily schedule to get your own work done. Otherwise, the requests and demands of all your stakeholders will quickly overwhelm every second of every day."

"You mean I need to delegate responsibility more."

He nodded. "That's half of it. But the people you delegate to will quickly begin to make their own demands on your attention. No, what I mean is that you need to reserve time strictly for *you*, and you alone."

"I'll remember that."

"I'm sure you will. But I'm not at all sure that you'll actually implement it."

"Why? You don't think I'm strong enough?"

"You wouldn't be the toast of the Valley right now if you weren't a very strong person. No, my concern is that you still want the people who work for you to like you. You still want them to be your friends. You think that to take time just for yourself is to be selfish. And to be selfish is to have those same employees starting thinking of you as—if you'll excuse the expression—a selfish *cunt*."

She was so surprised by the word that she blushed, then quickly tried to cover it. "You misjudge me, Arthur. You know as well as I do that I've already fired employees. That I've sued suppliers. And I've cancelled distribution contracts. Those aren't exactly the actions of the delicate flower you seem to think I am."

"Perhaps," he said. "And I watched you do each of those things, and, of course, your behavior was without reproach. But I also noticed that each time, you went to great pains to explain how the decision was not your fault, that it was out of your hands, that the victims deserved it."

He dipped a torn piece of ciabatta into a bulls-eye of olive oil and balsamic vinegar on a side plate, then put it into his mouth and chewed thoughtfully, as if phrasing in his mind the most succinct words of advice.

"Tell me," he asked, "what happens when one of these decisions *is* your fault? When you have to take the blame—and the hatred—of your 'friends' because it is the best of two bad choices? What happens when you have to fire someone who doesn't deserve it? You've never directed a mass lay-off in your entire career. Can you really pull the trigger on all those nice people who have worked so hard for you, who have mortgages and little babies at home, and who don't have much chance of finding another job in a long, long time?"

"I don't expect that to happen," said Alison. "Certainly not anytime soon. And when—and if—it does there are alternatives to just a single brutal lay-off. For example…"

Bellflower cut her off. "It will happen. Probably sooner than you think. And there won't be an alternative… not if you want your company to survive."

"Well, then, I'll do what has to be done."

"We'll see," he said. "Now, other than allowing me to play the old scold with you, why are we having lunch today?"

"Actually, Arthur, the fact is that I really did want to hear what you just told me. I hoped to get some last advice from you before your upcoming departure from the board. And I just wanted some private time with you, before all of the formal ceremonies that are coming up, to thank you personally for all of your help."

Arthur Bellflower sat back and looked at her for a long time. Alison thought she saw a small tear form in his eyes. But only for a moment.

"Alison, it was great pleasure and honor to work with you," he said. "As for thanking me, hell, I should be thanking you. You made my firm and its investors more than $400 million. That's enough to guarantee the success of that fund no matter what happens to all of our other investments. And the fact that Manzanita Capital is now synonymous with a superstar start-up like eTernity has enabled us to fully subscribe our new $2 billion fund in record time. And last but not least, your success has put a small fortune into my own pocket."

He smiled briefly. "But between you and me, the best part of working with you has been just the plain fun of being part of a hot new start-up company and helping turn it into a world-beater. I've had a lot of different jobs in my career, but not one has been nearly as much fun as this one. It's been an honor to work with you, Alison. You may be the best entrepreneur I've ever worked with."

"Well," she said, "the feeling is mutual, Arthur. Speaking as the CEO of eTernity, we couldn't have gotten this far without you. And speaking personally, I've come to think of you as one of my closest friends."

The waiter brought their meals. By the time she looked up from her plate of gnocchi, Alison was surprised to find the old venture capitalist looking at her with a stern face. "You are mistaken, my dear," he said. "I am *not* your friend. My friends are aging men who fish and play golf with me. They are the godfathers of my children, and I've known many of them since college. By comparison, young lady, you have never been to my house, nor I to your apartment. I'll bet you don't even know my wife's name, or the number of grandchildren I have."

Alison froze, the fork in her hand poised inches above her plate. She felt as if she'd been slapped in the face.

"What I've been," he continued, "is your business partner. And whether you appreciate it or not, I've been the most loyal and supportive partner you'll probably ever have. Early on, I went to bat for you when the other investors thought you weren't up for the job. For the last year, I've been assuring them that you have the ability to grow with the firm as it transforms from a spunky little start-up to a big, mature company. Just so you know, Alison, I don't usually take that position. On the contrary, I'm usually the investor who's the first to open the trap door on the founder."

"I didn't know all of that," she said slowly.

"You didn't need to," said Bellflower. "When I do my job right, the only thing you should notice is that there are no cliffs in your path."

"And the cliffs ahead?"

"You'll need other help with those. Or better yet, you need to learn to fly over them. You're further along in this process than I've ever been. You need a new mentor now. I suggest it not be a *friend*, but someone whose interests are more fiduciary—and therefore more pure—than mine have been. You need honesty, not sympathy."

"And you, Arthur? Will you still be there to advise me?"

"I will remain a major shareholder in eTernity. As long as that's the case, my advice is available to you anytime you need it. If I should sell my stock—or invest in a new competitor—that support will, of course, end." He smiled again. "On the other hand, when that day comes, perhaps we'll finally discuss becoming friends."

V. 5.7

After lunch, a slightly dazed Alison walked down University Avenue towards the parking lot and her new Mercedes. The car was her only indulgence, since she knew that any sale of stock reduced her control of the company. The sidewalks were crowded, with no sign of the predicted recession yet. She looked up and noticed the marquee of the Stanford Theater: "The Best Years of Our Lives" was showing, paired with "Executive Suite." In the jammed Apple Store, a knot of people swarmed around the display of the newest MacBook. And in the window of Francis Ford Coppola's restaurant, she recognized a notorious investment banker who'd nearly gone to prison, huddled in a deep conversation with an equally well-known magazine editor.

She needed to use the lock button on her keychain, with its resulting honk, to recognize her new car. As she climbed in, Alison checked her Blackberry. There was a text message from Jenny Randall, now eTernity's sales director, asking if Alison had time for a short meeting tomorrow. Starting the motor, she started to back out... then stopped. It struck her that she already knew what the meeting would be about.

She glanced up at herself in the mirror. Her face had grown tighter; the furrow between her eyes deeper, and the lines in the corners of her mouth were even more defined. She thought of reaching up and brushing back her hair, and perhaps putting on some lipstick. But her hands never left the steering wheel.

Will it be just me in the end? she asked herself. Are they all going to leave me—all those people who were supposed to be my friends, but in the end will prove to be just co-workers? And when the bleeding stops, will it be just me?

Probably.

But if that's so, she thought, *why haven't I followed the path of the others and left?*

Even as she asked the question, Alison knew the answer: *Because I have nothing else.*

V. 6.0

Tipo had just connected the plasma TV on the wall of Alison's new office. "Oh, look," he exclaimed, peering through the newly jet-black hair that draped over his eyes. "Satan's on tour."

Alison, who was lining up books on her credenza, turned to see. There on the screen, talking to Neil Cavuto, was Cosmo Validator. With his huge head, lined and tanned face, and pompadour of silver hair, he looked more leonine than ever. And that was appropriate, because the silky old legend was in the midst of announcing the creation of his new foundation dedicated to saving the giant sable antelope of Angola—no doubt, she thought ruefully, so he can get the chance to shoot one. The topic then turned to the political plans of Validator's wife… which Cosmo deftly deflected by saying only that Ms. Validator was fielding a number of requests to run for various offices.

"Turn it up," Alison said as she slipped into a new leather office chair that was still covered with plastic. She leaned forward with her chin in her hands to catch the nuances in Validator's expressions. What is he? she asked herself. Sixty-five? Seventy? God, he's still a very attractive man. An alpha of alphas. Repellent and sexy at the same time. And dangerous too. Thank heavens I don't have to compete directly against him: he'd have my stuffed head on the wall alongside his enemies and ex-wives.

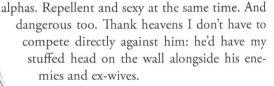

"It's been a rough year for your company, hasn't it Cosmo?" Cavuto was asking.

"We grow through adversity," came the predictable answer.

Did Cosmo just wink? Alison wondered. Now *that's* balls.

"Yes," said Cavuto, "but there are some who say that you brought this on yourself by announcing a major organizational change when you didn't need to. Wasn't that an unforced error?"

Validator smiled. "Better than having to change when you *do* need to. Desperation almost always leads to bigger errors."

"Yes, but Validator stock is in the tank. The company's numbers haven't met analysts' estimates in four quarters. And at the company's annual shareholder's meeting last week, your own hand-picked successor, Dan Crowen, offered nothing to make investors the least bit optimistic about the company's near future."

"Your point, Neil?" Cosmo asked, his eyes lidded.

"My point, Cosmo, is that even if your strategy is a good one—and that's far from certain—are you sure you have the right leadership in place at Validator Software to execute that strategy?"

Validator threw his head back, as if pondering how to respond to Cavuto's unexpected question. Then he leaned forward, and his craggy face and green eyes filled the screen. "Neil, I *believe* in the long-term prospects of my company... and I have full *faith* that Dan Crowen will get us there."

"Wow," said Tipo, who was sitting on the shrink-wrapped couch. "Did he just stand by Crowen, or did he just stab him in the back?"

"Maybe both," said Alison. "Now, shhh, listen."

"... about eTernity and its CEO, Alison Prue?" Cavuto said, finishing a question.

Validator smiled wryly. "You know I only say good things about my competitors."

Cavuto laughed. "You and I both know that's only been true in the breach."

Validator's expression didn't change. He looked like an amused Great White Shark. "I would have to say that Ms. Prue and her team have done a hell of a job... *to this point*... and they deserve every ounce of credit and reward they've received."

"Damn right," muttered Tipo.

"However," Cosmo continued, "as you well know, there's a vast gulf between the skills needed to run a new start-up company—something Ms. Prue has in spades—and those required to lead a large public corporation."

"I don't disagree," said Cavuto. "But you in turn must admit that she's been in the new job for a year now... and it seems to have gone without a hitch."

"So far," said Validator inscrutably. "And I'm sure she and her team feel like they can accomplish anything right now. But they're heading into some major challenges for which they're mostly unprepared."

Cavuto seemed surprised at the man's bluntness. "Care to elaborate?"

"No," said Validator, his smile firmly in place. "But as my mother used to say to me as a boy, 'Time will tell.'"

Alison shivered. It was as if Cosmo Validator could smell her fear.

V. 6.1

A lone in his office, Dan Crowen watched the interview on the display of his computer. It ran in a box in the upper right hand corner with the weekly sales numbers on the rest of the screen. The interview had begun as a typical Cosmo Validator charm session, so Dan's attention shifted back to the numbers. But when he heard his own name, he quickly switched the interview to the main screen. That's when he heard Validator say, "… full *faith…*" in a manner that suggested just the opposite.

"You son of a bitch," Dan said aloud. "You create this clusterfuck, you expect me to make it work—and now, just when I'm finally turning things around, you saw me off at the knees? All so that the mighty Cosmo Validator can take credit if it works, and shift the blame to me if it doesn't."

"So, tell me, Cosmo," asked Cavuto, "is all of this upheaval at Validator at an end? Will we now see a return to normalcy at Validator Software?"

Validator rocked his head slightly, as if trying to minimize his answer. "Not quite yet. There's one more comparatively minor downsizing that's about to take place. That should do it."

The interview went on for another two minutes, but Dan heard nothing else after that. He spun his seat around and stared out the window at the small Japanese garden. *How does he know that?* he asked himself. And the realization hit him like a gut punch.

By the time he turned back to his desk, the interview had been replaced by commercials. He cleared the image and called up Instant Message. "I need to talk to you immediately," he typed. "In my office."

Less than a minute later, there was a knock on the door. "Come in," said Dan. He didn't stand as Lisa walked in. She walked over to take the sole chair on the side of the desk, as she had many times before.

"No need to sit," Dan said peremptorily. She seemed surprised, then her face became an expressionless mask, and she stood, feet together and hands folded in front of her.

"You asked for me?" she asked in a flat tone.

He studied her for a moment: the cold eyes, the sharp features... *how did I ever see her as pretty?* he wondered. "Cosmo just ratted you out," he told her. "You're finished. I want you out of here by five tonight."

She didn't react. "May I have a ride to the Jetport?"

"Take a cab," he snapped. "And bill Cosmo for the... *service.*"

She nodded slightly. "Anything else?"

There were so many things Dan wanted to say, so many words he wanted to throw at this woman and her boss. Then it struck him that the smart strategy was to not show his cards just yet.

"No."

She nodded again. "Mr. Validator has asked me to tell you that you have two quarters to show positive results for your efforts—or he will find someone who can."

Dan forced himself not to react. "Message received." He locked eyes with her, and didn't take his eyes off her until the door closed behind her.

When she was gone, he hurled himself out of his chair and began to pace the room. Thoughts and arguments and accusations raced through his brain too quickly to settle on any single one. After thirty minutes of angry insanity, and another fifteen minutes of surfing the Web to plumb the business world's reactions to Cosmo's latest remarks, he found himself outside, sitting on a cold stone bench in the Japanese garden. The soft spectrum of greens and the precisely trimmed borders cooled the raging fire in his brain and reasserted an order to his thoughts.

He could hear cars in the parking lot just beyond the bamboo screen. *If they weren't watching that interview,* he told himself, *they've all undoubtedly heard about it by now. How am I going to walk out and face them all—and ask them to trust me and make even more sacrifices—when all 32,000 of them now know that the beloved founder and chairman of the board has lost faith in me? How can I convince them all to follow me, when everyone from the janitors to my own executive team now assumes I'm a short-timer?*

He shivered slightly in the cold, but he didn't move. A tiny bird hopped out from under a boxwood bush and up onto a nearby juniper plant, where it began to tear off the dusty blue berries, apparently in pursuit of just the right one. Eventually, the bird noticed the large figure on the nearby bench. It stopped and stared, turning its head one way, then the other. Dan made a clicking sound with his tongue... and the little bird, almost comically, fluttered back under the boxwood for safety.

He took a deep breath that seemed to revive him. What have I got to lose now, but everything? The hyperbole of the words made him chuckle out loud. Still, it was true—and the words were somehow liberating. If he was going to fail anyway, then why not go down fighting for what he believed in?

But what *did* he believe in? Dan was astonished—his jaw actually dropped—to realize that he already knew: he still believed in Validator Software. Even more amazing, he would willingly *die* to make it a success again... a company that bore the name of the man who had just betrayed him.

And also, he realized—with far less surprise—there was something else he would die for.

V. 6.2

t was late, and the line of headlights across the Bay Bridge had thinned enough for the cars to drive at the speed limit. Alison could just make them out in the reflection of herself standing at the whiteboard in the nearly empty conference room. It's a good thing there's nothing fourteen stories tall between here and the Bay, she thought, because what I'm writing could make somebody quite rich.

There was a magnum bottle of Two-Buck Chuck merlot on the counter by the sink, along with a toppled stack of Styrofoam cups. She poured herself a half-cup and sat down at the chair that she'd placed ten feet in front of the whiteboard. She took a sip—*God, this is terrible stuff,* she thought—then sat back and studied what she'd written.

Emerging from the pentimento of a half-dozen failed attempts and erasures was half of an organization chart. Manufacturing, customer service, sales, marketing, and marketing communications were in place—but not yet R&D, finance, or HR. Most important, the upper levels of management, and the people to fill them, were done. She had worked on those first.

She studied the titles and names in the upper regions of the chart. An understanding had been quietly growing in her over the last few weeks that having most of the eTernity start-up team quit—so painful at first—was going to be a blessing in disguise. All those newly-emptied slots had freed her to raise to those executive positions a new group of stronger and more experienced managers. Most of them would never have survived the disorganization and improvisation of eTernity's early days. But all were perfectly suited for the rough and tumble of global competition and corporate politics. If she could hold them together, they'd make a potent team.

She took another drink of bad wine. *Here I come, Cosmo...*

V. 6.3

Primroses had been planted along the walk from the driveway to the house. And there was now an elegant little fountain in the center of the koi pond in front of the guest house. Dan was disheveled and his head was bowed, but he registered each change as he passed. Each was a reminder of how long he'd been gone. How much life had been lived here without his presence?

He climbed the front steps. A line of new ceramic pots, each filled with a different lily, ran up the steps beside him. In the entryway, a new teak bench had replaced the old wrought iron one they'd bought at an antique shop in SoHo before Aiden was born. He paused on the threshold, caught his breath, straightened his hair and tie, then rang the doorbell.

After a few moments, the handle clicked and the door opened. Annabelle, in her gardening clothes and wearing a scarf, was as beautiful as Dan had ever seen her. She looked surprised to see him. She brightened with recognition, then caught herself. "Don't you still have a key?" she asked.

"Yes," Dan said, "but I felt I needed your permission to enter. I have something I want to say to you."

V. 7.0

The swelling and waning of the roar of the crowd on the far side of the curtains reminded Alison of waves on a shingle beach. Tony D. was standing beside her. He was the new eTernity VP of Sales, and he would be introduced to the shareholders today.

He raised a fist. "Reminds me of an Apple event."

"Great," said Alison. "As long as they aren't expecting me to be Steve Jobs."

He grinned. "You've got much better legs."

She forced a grim smile. She'd been warned that suffering through Tony D.'s banter would be the cost of getting a great sales director—and sticking it in Validator's eye.

She looked around. Backstage was filled with excited young people, all of them eTernity employees. Only a few of them had been with the company more than four months. They all knew how lucky they were to be part of the most exciting company of the moment... and all felt that they more than deserved it.

It was so different from just a year ago. The team was all amateurs then, smart but inexperienced, and making it up as they went along. Now most of them were gone, taking their riches and heading off to live out their dreams. This *is* my dream, isn't it? Alison asked herself.

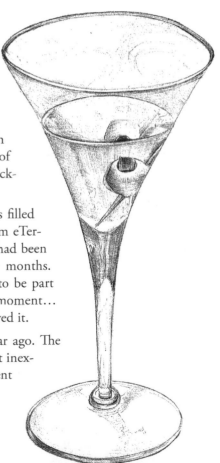

She studied the backstage crowd. All of them were pros; there wasn't a neophyte in the group... well, thought Alison, except maybe me. She spotted a woman—slim, crisply dressed in a business suit, short blonde hair—holding a clipboard in one hand and a stopwatch in the other. She was the event organizer, the best in the business, they said, and her job was to organize the entertainment and set the schedule, and then to make sure that schedule was followed to the minute.

The woman, who probably knew where Alison was at every moment, caught her eye for instant, nodded, then studiously looked away. She's probably been told not to speak directly to me, Alison realized.

Alison found it all a bit unsettling. But then, wasn't that what big successful companies did? They found strength in their size and their organization, and they timed their actions to the second.

She heard music, and the roar of the audience swelled again: the five-minute slide show prelude had begun. How they found that much content for a company this young remained a mystery to her. But Alison also knew that it didn't much matter. This crowd had come to celebrate, and nothing was going to divert them. And, in fact, the cheers had already begun.

And why not? The stock had climbed 700 percent since the IPO, which had not only made those shareholders out there a lot of money, but also gave them the social cachet of being able to say they'd been with eTernity from the start. That made them brilliant investors—and there was nothing better in tech than to be perceived as a genius.

The folks standing about chatting and laughing backstage were delirious, too. For sheer social power, the only thing that trumped investing in the hottest company of the decade was to work for that company. Whatever the future brought, the employees knew that to have this era's eTernity on their resumé would put a fine glow on the rest of their careers. The world would assume they were the best in their profession, that they were smart and clever... and most of all, that they were *lucky*.

None of them would notice—not yet at least, because the information was still internal—but there was already a lot that kept Alison awake even more than usual at night.

The core product line was still as strong and popular as ever. But several of the add-on applications had been met with mixed reviews from both reviewers and customers. Meanwhile, Version 2.0, which was promised for introduction six months from now, had already begun to slip. There was real doubt they'd hit even that intentionally generous delivery date; they might be as much as three months late.

Rumors of that fact had in turn begun to worry company vendors. After all, they had dropped their safe, proven Validator partnerships to take the risk of adopting the popular new eTernity standard their customers had demanded. They weren't freaking out yet, but Alison sensed they were beginning to wonder if they'd made a dangerous mistake. Perhaps the word was getting out too, because the torrid pace of the stock price had begun to slow. Most analysts thought it was temporary, but maybe it was more.

And that was just the product. Alison knew there were some internal problems at eTernity. So did the rest of the company, though most of them dismissed it as 'growing pains' that Prue and her team would fix. One vice-president, formerly a well-regarded lab director at a Fortune 50 company, had joined eTernity... and quit two months later to go back his old employer. The official story was that the giant company had offered him a king's ransom to return. But Alison knew how much salary and stock she'd offered to get him to join eTernity—and she knew he would have stayed if he'd felt comfortable working at the new company.

Even worse, she'd decided that the costs of success might be outweighing the costs of failure. She thought back to that night when she'd sat at that whiteboard and reorganized the company. Like a good technologist, she had focused on the part of the company that designed and sold and serviced the company's products. Why had she assumed that Human Resources would take care of itself? Why hadn't she made hiring of the rank-and-file of the company as much of a priority as her own recruiting of senior management?

Now she had a mess on her hands. Like every hot tech company—and these days eTernity was a supernova—it had initially been buried in thousands of job applications. HR had managed to hire the best and brightest (and youngest) of these applicants, but it had taken too damn long. In fact, the hiring was still going on.

And that was only the start. Once those legions of newcomers arrived at eTernity, they soon discovered that HR had almost no place to put them, much less assimilate them into the company's culture. New hires camped out in offices with no furniture, taking jobs that as yet had no description. Much more dangerous, these new hires had naturally filled the cultural void with the one they had brought from their last employer.

In an older company with established patterns and a body of corporate legends, that wouldn't have been too bad, but in a young company like eTernity, with a fragile and still incomplete sense of itself, the organization quickly began to divide into different camps—the Validator crowd (the product of successful raids on that company's former sales staff), the Twillium crowd, and the very dangerous Google crowd. They were all pulling the company in different directions to impose their own personality on the organization.

The problem would be fixed eventually. Alison had fired the HR director. It had been the first major firing of her career, and it would have gone worse if she hadn't kept Arthur Bellflower's words in her head. The woman had walked out of the company with $10 million in her pocket for five months of incompetence—thanks to Alison's mistake of giving her vested shares on hiring. But at least she was gone. And the new HR director, a veteran from Hewlett-Packard, had already begun to assert control. Fortunately, those HP guys really knew corporate culture and new employee orientation.

But there were still pockets of competing cultures, nowhere more than in the newly created sales force. Alison had been told that Tony D. was an oversized personality, but that wasn't the half of it. Unconstrained, he'd formed the sales department in his own image, one very different from the rest of the company.

She glanced over at Tony D. He caught the glance and grinned. "They're pissing on themselves out there. This is going to be a goddamn coronation."

She smiled, nodded, and turned away. *We'll cross the Tony D. bridge when we come to it.*

There was a tap on her shoulder. She turned to see the event organizer standing beside her. "One minute, Ms. Prue," the woman said. Alison nodded. The woman remained beside her, looking down at the stopwatch—now attached to the clipboard—and adjusting her earpiece.

Enjoy this, Alison told herself. *Who knows when it will be this great again? I just need to emphasize the profits. A great profit margin means money in the bank—and that money can cover a lot of mistakes. It's a cushion for hard times. It'll enable us to hire more codewriters to get that damn 2.0 version out on time. And the stock market loves cash. Just keep talking about that—the rest will take care of itself.*

The woman flicked the switch on the battery pack attached to the small of Alison's back, then stepped in front of her to grab the edge of the curtain. "Three," she said, "Two... One..."

Tony D. gave her a hearty thumbs up. The curtains were pulled back. Alison saw a sea of faces and brilliant lights. The crowd roared.

V. 7.1

D an poked his head into the office doorway of his COO, Bert Hamlin. "How did she do?" he asked. "I had a conference call."

Bert looked up from his computer screen. He had the face of confident raptor. "Not over yet, but I think she's done."

"And... ?"

"Not bad. Not great. She was visibly nervous at the beginning." He fluttered his hands in front of his face. "She did a lot of stuff with her hands for the first half of the speech, but she finally got that under control."

Dan nodded. "Anything else?"

"No verbal gaffes. No big surprises—other than yet another confirmation that their follow-up product is running late."

"She admitted that?"

"Not exactly. It was more of a case of omission. She stopped talking about delivery dates a month ago—and if she was going to set a new date, this would have been the moment to do so."

"Did she take questions?"

"No. The crowd was too big for that kind of thing. But they would have softballed it anyway. By all the applause and cheering, it was obvious that everybody was on her side. If someone had even tried a tough question, they probably would have gotten lynched right there on the spot."

"Must be nice," Dan said. "Any sign of Tony D.?"

"Yep. He was the same as always—which was kind of weird with that crowd. Kind of like your rich, white-shoed uncle trying to be hip in a room full of twenty-somethings. Which is basically what it was. That's probably why they only gave him a couple minutes and got him off the stage fast."

"Poor Tony."

"I wouldn't say that," Bert said. "He's got the best sales job in tech. He's going to be richer than he already is. And he gave the impression of being in charge—and a grown-up—which may not have worked with the crowd, but you can damn well bet it comforted all those institutional investors out there."

"So, in summary," Dan said, "Prue *survived.* But she doesn't look like a confident corporate chief executive yet. The shareholders are still wildly enthusiastic. Sales look healthy and the salesforce is under experienced management, but that department's style is nearly antithetical to the rest of the company. And the big follow-up product may be slipping. Does that about cover it?"

"You got it."

"I think we can work with that," said Dan. "Don't you?"

Bert smiled. "Yes, I do. I don't think we can beat them yet. But if that product slips by more than three months, I think we might catch them."

V. 7.2

Alison groaned, kicked off her shoes, and lay back on her office couch. Thank God that's over, she thought. Her feet hurt, her back hurt, and the three Advils she'd taken were only beginning to dampen her splitting headache.

It hadn't gone too badly. She'd lapsed into her usual nervous hands thing, but caught it early and stopped. And she'd very nearly lost it when the demonstration program had failed to boot up on the first try. Luckily, she'd kept her composure, vamped, even told a lame joke—and, just in time, the file successfully opened.

It must have worked, she told herself, because the crowd was still chanting and cheering as much at the end of her speech as they had been at the beginning. Better yet, the stock had held steady all day, even closing up a dollar per share…

"Ms. Prue?"

She opened her eyes to see James, her new secretary, standing over her. The light in the room had changed since she closed her eyes. "Ma'am. It's six o'clock. I believe you have an engagement this evening."

Alison sat up slowly. Her back throbbed, and now her neck was stiff. "I must have dozed off."

"You looked very tired, ma'am. So I'm sure you needed it."

"Anybody try to contact me?"

"Quite a few people, but mostly to offer congratulations. Same with the emails. You got a very nice one from Mr. Bellflower, which I've tagged for you."

"Thank you."

"Otherwise, I basically told everybody you were doing media interviews."

"Well done, James," she said. His face brightened. "Now go home. You've had a long day."

"Thank you, Ma'am. I've put the name of the gentleman and the address of the restaurant on a post-it note on your desk."

An hour later, she had refreshed her make-up and lipstick and brushed her hair, but was still wearing her work clothes. She was sitting across from "Fredrick, but please call me Fred"—a stockbroker with a loud voice and a receding hairline—at a table in Alfred's. It was an old steakhouse with white tablecloths and red walls, old paintings, and tuck-and-rolled booth backs.

"... Yeah, one of the perquisites of being a Yalie is that I get to stay at the various Harvard-Yale clubs around the world—or, if not that, in one of the other university clubs that have a reciprocal relationship with mine. It's the only way to go. You went to Stanford, right? I think I read that on your Wikipedia page."

"Yes."

"Well, the Farm is sort of like an Ivy League school, now, isn't it? I bet they've got clubs too. You ought to look into it."

"I will," she said.

"So I saw that you had your annual meeting today. Sounds like it went really well."

"I think so."

"And I read the transcripts from your analyst phone call."

"Did you? I thought you specialized in semiconductors."

"Oh, I do. But you know. I knew we were going to meet tonight, and so I thought I'd do a little *client research*, if you know what I mean."

"Ah."

Fred leaned forward and lowered his voice. "So as long as we're having a private dinner together, I was wondering if you had any idea yet when you're going to get that new product out the door?"

V. 7.3

It was a long drive from the Denver airport north to Loveland, then up the Big Thompson canyon into the Rockies towards Estes Park. Dan and Annabelle checked into the Inn at Glen Haven, took a short nap, and then drove out Devils Gulch Road to the Center. It had been crisp and windy in Loveland, but at this higher altitude, it was cold. Occasional snowflakes melted on the windshield as the car hissed down the wet road.

A high fence topped with barbed wire encircled the compound, which was itself little more than a half-dozen prefab buildings, a couple trailers, and a large pole barn. There were already more than twenty cars, almost all of them obvious rentals, parked in front of the headquarters building, which sported a flagpole and a carved wooden sign that read "Wilderness Rehabilitation."

Annabelle pulled her fur collar tighter around her neck. Her face looked pale and drawn and her eyes blurred with tears. "It looks like a prison," she said.

"It is. In a way," said Dan. "But there are a lot of cars. At least we're not the only people in this mess."

"I just want to see her," said Annabelle. "I need to see her face and hear her voice."

From the headquarters, they joined a knot of several dozen middle aged people, all bundled against the cold, all looking both hopeful and fearful, and all trying to evade eye contact with the others. Together, they were led to a second, even larger building that wore a hand-painted welcome sign over its entrance. Few of the visitors even noticed the sign; they simply trudged forward, resolutely looking at the soggy ground, several couples huddling against each other.

The double doors opened to a brightly lit cafeteria. Streamers and hand-made paper snowflakes hung from the ceiling lights. The two long lines of tables had been draped in red and green wrapping paper and decorated with candles, pine cones, and sprigs of holly and cedar. From a table along a side wall, an iPod pumped out Christmas music through a beat-up pair of speakers.

At the far end of the room stood a group of young people, all wearing Santa Claus stocking caps and intently watching the new arrivals. As soon as the parents entered the room, this group quickly made its way down the long aisle between the tables, smiling and picking up the pace as they went.

Aidan stopped in front of her parents and gave a small wave. "Hi, guys."

"Oh honey," Annabelle whispered and wrapped her daughter in a hug. Dan, feeling his own burning tears threatening to spill, wrapped his arms around the pair.

Aidan escorted her parents to a pair of chairs with their names on the placemats, then left to get them coffee ("We drink gallons of the stuff around here—standard druggies, looking for any high") and cookies ("No rum balls, of course"). As she left, Annabelle turned to Dan. "What do you think? She sure looks a lot better."

"She does," he agreed. "She seems a whole lot tougher, too."

"She probably has to be to make it in a place like this."

"Where did she get the nose ring?"

"I'm not even going to ask. Let's just win this big battle first."

The director of the program offered a brief welcome over a tinny loud-speaker. He was careful to remind both the 'students' and the parents that this was only the first step of many months of additional treatment before the families could be reunited permanently. He introduced the staff ("She's my counselor," said Aidan when one heavyset woman with the face of a Sunday School teacher was introduced) and then, understanding the real reason for the day, quickly ended the program. The sound level of the room instantly rose as seated figures huddled into separate knots, everyone rushing to bring each other up to date.

The room grew even louder and stuffier, and Aidan suggested that she take her parents on a tour of the facility. Snow began falling more heavily as she pointed out her dorm building, the equipment house, and the nurse's office. "It's no big deal," she told them, "because most of the last two months we've been up there." She pointed towards the peaks that towered above them.

"That's a relief," said Annabelle, "because this place reminds me too much of a prison."

"Oh," said Aidan, gesturing for them to sit beside her on a painted wooden bench. "You mean the fences? Actually, they're there as much to keep people out as to keep us in."

"Why would anybody want in?" Dan asked her.

"Oh, you know: horny boyfriends, junkie girlfriends needing money, dealers looking for squealers, that kind of thing. Frankly, there's some people who'd like to find me, too. Luckily, I'm in Colorado, not California."

Annabelle began to cry again. "Oh honey. I'm so sorry for everything."

"It wasn't your fault, mom," Aidan said, taking her mother's hand. "If there's one lesson they teach you here it's that it's your own damn fault. Nobody else's."

"I don't understand," said Dan. "How did you get in this deep without us catching you? We knew you were having some problems, but until you got... arrested... we had no idea it was so bad."

"Oh," Aidan replied, "that's more common than you think, dad. I'll bet you most of the parents here today had no idea until everything blew up in their faces. They teach us about that here, too: you don't see what you don't believe." She squeezed her mother's hand and snuggled closer to her. "Mom knew something was wrong. But I knew that she would always believe the best about me."

"And me?" asked Dan.

Aidan looked into her father's eyes with a fearlessness he had never seen in her before. "You were easy, because you weren't there."

As she watched her parents' heads bow, Aidan sensed that she had gone too far. "Come on, guys, it's all okay now. I made my own choices and now I'm dealing with them. I'm just lucky you could afford to pay for all this good treatment. And that I have a nice house to come home to."

V. 7.4

Five hundred half-drunk employees and their mates combined with a live band made a lot of noise, especially in the glass amplifier of the Market Street Galleria. Alison stood on stage between the members of the Tokyo Police Club and shook a tambourine. She could feel the roar bouncing off the walls and hammering back at her like a staccato of explosions. When the band abruptly stopped, her ears continued to ring.

Someone handed her a microphone. The crowd was cheering now. "Happy holidays, everybody!" she shouted to a blast of feedback. Someone turned down the gain on the speaker. "Is everybody having fun? It's been a heckuva year, hasn't it?" The crowd roared with each question.

Alison introduced the band. She introduced the employee of the year. She introduced the vice-mayor of San Francisco, who—hoping for support on a new anti-fast food initiative—had agreed to represent the City at the event. With each introduction, the crowd cheered. Then she called up Reverend Cecil Williams, an aging black man in a dark suit and African scarf, to accept a $50,000 check for the Glide Memorial soup kitchen. Next, she reached into a goldfish bowl held by hipster-dressed Tipo and pulled out the name of the winner of the company's $150,000 employee raffle: a stunned young Pakistani woman who'd only been at eTernity for five weeks.

Finally, the big moment: the annual Christmas bonus. Alison played it like an Academy Award. A representative from Price Waterhouse in a suit and sunglasses appeared from the wings and delivered an envelope. She took it, opened it, peered inside… and then appeared to be on the brink of fainting. The crowd roared. Pretending to be frightened, she peeked into the envelope again. The crowd was shouting now. Then she smiled, pulled out the card and showed the number to the crowd. "One hundred twenty-seven percent!" she shouted.

Pandemonium. After a year in which most of the crowd had found a job at the hottest company in the industry, and in which they had been offered a future fortune in stock, now they were each to be awarded a bonus equal to more than their biweekly paycheck. There were high-fives, backs slapped, hugs, and kisses that lasted a little too long.

"One. Two. Three!" Alison shouted, and the band broke into "Nature of the Experiment." Alison handed off the microphone and fled the stage.

It seemed to take forever to wend her way through the crowd; more than ever, everyone wanted to congratulate her, thank her, touch her. Exhausted and battered, she at last found the bar in the back of the hall. There were some small tables set up there, and though most were full, she saw Tony D. sitting alone nursing a martini. He stood and gestured for her to join him. "Saved it for you. I knew you'd need it."

"It's nice to work with someone who's been through all of this before," she said as she took a chair.

"Many times," he said, "but not quite like this. I don't know if there's ever been anything quite like this."

Alison shook a random congratulating hand. "And Happy Holidays to you," she said, searching for the man's name, and failing. "Thanks for all that you've done."

She turned back to Tony D. and shook her head. "I honestly don't know who that was. Is he an employee?"

Tony D. shrugged.

"You know, it's crazy," she said. "Just a year ago there were only a dozen of us. I knew everybody's name—their kids, their lovers, their hobbies, what kind of coffee they drank. Now we've got five hundred employees, and I'll bet I still don't know more than a dozen of them well... and half of them are survivors from the old days."

Tony D. looked over the rim of his glass at her. "Well, get used to it. Hell, I'm in the business of knowing names. But long ago I learned that when in doubt you call all women 'Honey' and all men 'Champ.'"

"Sounds unpromising," said Alison. *What a repulsive man.*

"Whatever. All I know is that you'd better prepare yourself." He waved his hand at the dancing crowd. "Because five years from now there may be ten thousand people out there you don't know. That's what happened at Validator."

Alison's eyes narrowed. She leaned in his direction. "You know... *Tony*... you and I have never really talked about your days at Validator Software.

Now that you've been here six months, I don't think we'll be violating any non-competition clauses to finally have a little conversation about the place."

He winked at her. "What do you want to know, kid?"

She gave him a sexy smile. "Tell me about Cosmo Validator... No, tell me about Dan Crowen first. Tell me all about him."

Tony made a great display of glancing about conspiratorially, then turned back to her with a lascivious look in his eyes. This was going to be fun.

V. 8.0

The wind and rain were blowing so hard that Dan seriously wondered if the ball he was about to putt might stop short of the cup... and then be blown right back to his putter. For the first time he fully understood the meaning of a 'horizontal storm.'

Bandon Dunes was proving to be everything he had heard it would be, a classic Scottish Links on the Southern Oregon coast. On the sixteenth green he'd looked south through the driving rain to see the superstructure of a huge dredge rocking in the channel of the Coquille River, just yards from the famous little lighthouse. It was made perfect by what would be, Stevenson had said on the phone, "the worst fucking weather imaginable. You are going to be wet; you are going to be freezing ass cold; and you are going to have the greatest goddamn round of your life."

Now, the four of them—all Dartmouth Class of 1981—stood around the eighteenth green, awaiting their putts, with the wind and rain turning their foul weather gear into pennants and the golfers in the clubhouse bar above them looking down in envy. Donnie Watters, who was out, bent over his putter. Suddenly he looked up and shouted, "Ain't this a hell of thing? Why don't we all just retire and do this forever?"

Now the rain had stopped, but not the wind, and as Dan walked up Bandon Beach, he reminded himself to head north up the beach into the wind on his way out the next time. That way he'd have the wind at his back on the tired walk back. As the foam boiled up the flat beach, and the low gray clouds streamed overhead, he trudged up the wet sand with his hands in his pockets,   bent forward i n t o t h e gusts.

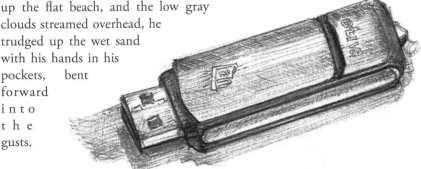

The great rock monoliths on the beach and just out into the water—so familiar from television commercials and magazine ads—were taking a beating from winter storm waves. Up ahead at Strawberry Point, the great hump of Grave Rock, with its sinister cave openings, was hit so hard by a wave that Dan could feel the booming report. He watched a column of foam blast up the rock's flank fifty feet into the air, like a whale spouting.

Just before the point, he turned inland. The sand wasn't as wet here, and the going was slower. A phalanx of sandpipers skittered away across the dune at his approach. He searched the low sand cliff for the gap in the wall of yellow-flowered gorse that ran up the steep hillside. There.

He climbed the cliff at a point where it collapsed and disappeared into the wall of green stickers. He emerged, panting hard, a hundred feet up the hillside on a steep path that had been cut through a thick blackberry patch. The path of slick green grass was dotted with banana slugs, and he did his best to navigate around them.

At last he climbed a set of wooden stairs and found himself on level ground. A manicured carpet of lawn spread out before him, leading to a redwood deck and a two-story vacation home. Above him, behind a big sixteen-light balcony window, sat Annabelle, wrapped in a robe and sitting in a rocking chair. She had on her reading glasses and was knitting a scarf for Aidan. She saw him on the lawn below and waved. He saluted back.

Two hours later, the wind and clouds had disappeared, leaving an astonishingly quiet beach, clear skies, and a cold, crisp breeze. Dan and Annabelle bundled up in their down jackets, grabbed two chairs and a bottle of Willamette wine and two juice glasses, and went out on the patio to watch the sunset. As always on the Oregon coast, it promised to be spectacular—but also, as always, it was rarely actually visible.

As the sky banded orange, pink, and salmon, and the ball of the sun turned red—revealing a tiny smear of fog on the distant horizon—they clicked glasses to their survival against all odds.

"I've been thinking," Dan said.

"I noticed," said Annabelle.

"You've always said that you'd love to take a cruise around the world."

"I do remember saying that."

He turned to look at her. "Then let's do it. We'll take a year. And we'll bring Aiden with us. Spend some time together."

She stared at him, started to laugh, then caught herself, "You're serious."

"Deadly so," said Dan. "Just give me six months. From today."

Annabelle looked out at the sunset for a long time. Then she reached over with her glass and tapped his. "Deal."

V. 8.1

I t certainly is an elegant restaurant, Dan thought as he nursed an iced tea and picked at his half-eaten lunch. But then, he hadn't expected anything less. Empty, too. He turned around to a sea of empty tables. Not a single person had come in since he sat down. The very pretty young hostess, looking awkward in her long dress, slumped at the reservation desk. And there wasn't even the sound of clanging pots coming from the kitchen. He went back to reading his Napa Visitor's Guide.

A voice beside him said, "Dan Crowen. Damn if it isn't you. I thought I'd seen a ghost when you walked in."

He looked up to see Armstrong Givens, late of eTernity, tanned and elegantly dressed in an open shirt and ascot. "Armstrong," he said, standing and shaking the man's hand. "How long has it been?"

"Too long, Daniel," said Givens. "What? Fifteen years? Back when you let me work out of the Validator booth at Comdex. Back before we became competitors to the death."

"Well, I hope we're still friends. Join me."

Armstrong sat down, leaned back, crossed both his arms and his legs, and studied Dan for a moment. "Just a chance visit?" he asked.

Dan smiled. "You do look good, Armstrong. How come I'm so much older and you never age a day?"

Armstrong gave him a shrewd look. "Because my Robert isn't as reasonable in his expectations as your Annabelle is." He finally unfolded. Resting his arms on the table, he leaned forward and confided, "Christ, Dan, I would love for once to act my age." He glanced down at Dan's plate. "I see you've attempted today's special."

"Yes," said Dan. "Quite good."

"Liar. The truth is that despite my many successful years in business, it never crossed my mind that it isn't enough to dream about opening a four star restaurant, or even to actually sink much of your fortune in that restaurant—but that you actually have to deliver a four star meal. And that, I'm afraid, is beyond the ability of my dear Robert." Givens put a hand to his heart. "My only defense is that I was blinded by love."

"So hire a top-notch chef. You've got the money. And you could probably find a half-dozen to steal in just this block alone."

"True," said Givens. "But keep in mind, the dream was for Robert to *be* a chef, not for Robert to *hire* a chef. I'm afraid my only choice now is between a fire sale and fire insurance. And given the state of the real estate market right now…"

"Do you miss the Valley?" Dan interrupted. "Do you miss the game?"

Armstrong looked away, out over the lonely restaurant. "My public position on that is that I am well out of it and contentedly enjoying my not-so hard-earned wealth. Privately—and I would only say this to you, Daniel—I miss it right down to the very core of my being. I thought this elegant thousand-dollar-cowboy-boot-in-a-1951-Chevy-pickup winemaking milieu perfectly fitted my sensibilities… and I could not have been more wrong. What I've learned about myself—and what, of course, you already knew about me, which is why you are here—is that I'm a killer at heart. And there's nothing I like more than a good fight-to-the-death business war."

"Even against old friends?"

Armstrong turned back and looked Dan in the eyes. "I fought you, didn't I? And I daresay I won. So, could I be just as ruthless against a sweet little girl who used to bring me cough drops when I had a cold? Oh, *fuck* yes."

Dan gave the tiniest of smiles. "Any possible conflicts? Stock? Options?"

"Well, happily—or unhappily, depending on your perspective—I liquidated all of my holdings in eTernity buying Robert's dream house just up the road. Most of the rest I poured down the grease trap here. And what few shares remained I sold off a couple months ago when I realized that eTernity was starting to stumble. Luckily the market hadn't noticed yet; it still hasn't. But it will. Do you agree?"

Dan nodded. "ETernity hasn't tried to lure you back?"

"No. But that isn't surprising. They're still in that phase where any of the pre-IPO founders are an affront to those who run the company now. But Daniel, you still haven't given me a good reason to take a job at Validator. If I wanted to spend my time with dinosaurs, I'd rent *Jurassic Park.*"

"I'm not talking about Validator proper," Dan replied. "I'm talking about a little independent side project."

Armstrong stared at him for a moment, then clapped his hands and shouted. "A skunkworks! A bloody skunkworks!" The bored hostess looked up, and then went back to her daydreams. Givens chuckled, then grew serious. "Daniel, correct me if I'm wrong, but don't you currently have a small job running a multi-billion dollar public corporation... ?"

"True."

"...and, *entre nous*, aren't we a little too old for that kind of thing?"

"Well, *I* am," said Dan. "But look at you: you're still a young man."

Now Armstrong really laughed.

"And besides..." Dan raised one eyebrow and pointed at the half-eaten food on his plate.

"Ah, yes."

"Robert might even like going home."

Armstrong caught Dan's eye and winked. "I think I may just leave Robert here."

V. 8.2

The iPad, sitting upright in its stand and serving as an alarm clock, clicked its huge display numbers to '5:30.' The image was replaced with a video of Irving Berlin dressed in a doughboy uniform singing "Oh, How I Hate to Get Up in the Morning."

Alison, swathed in warm sleep, forced herself to sit up. The new penthouse was still dark. Through the windows, the City seemed suspended in sleep, the Bay beyond black and bottomless.

She reached over and shook the sleeping figure beside her.

The young man was exotically handsome, his arms covered with tribal tattoos. He was a decade younger than Alison, a barista at a local coffee bar. He groaned and tried to turn over and return to sleep. She shook him again.

"Jesus. Why are we getting up so early?" he complained.

"I told you last night. I have an important—thing—at the office."

"Okay, so? I'll lock the place up when I leave."

"No," she said firmly. She climbed out of bed and wrapped herself in a robe. "You leave the place with me. And I lock the door behind us. Now get up. Make some coffee for yourself when you get to work."

"Drive me there?" the young man asked plaintively.

"Sure. Except for, you know, the last block."

"You're the boss," sighed the naked man. Scratching himself, he headed off for the guest bathroom.

"Yes, I am," Alison said under her breath.

An hour later she was sitting in the boardroom with four of her vice-presidents, each of them thumbing through their respective prepared scripts. In the corner sat Tipo, who now sported a buzz cut and a bow tie. He was armed with a computer and head-set and talking with the organizer of this quarterly call with the stock analysts—now a small army—who followed eTernity. "Okay, thank you," he said, then turned to the group. "Folks, if you'll put on your headsets, we'll begin in one minute."

This was Alison's fifth analyst call—and though she wasn't yet comfortable with them, she was no longer intimidated. She had learned that there was a kabuki-like quality to the experience. Her job, and that of her lieutenants, was to read from a carefully prepared script—and the analysts' job was to ask questions that were just probing enough to gain some additional information… but not enough to clue in their competitors or piss off eTernity and risk losing access. The real questions would be asked privately, later. From those conversations, plus a lot of additional research, each analyst would develop an estimate on the health of the company—and a prediction on the future of its stock.

There was a click in Alison's ear, and she heard the skillful phrases of welcome from the host of the call. He would guide them through the process, providing cues for each speaker and setting up the subsequent Q&A.

"I'd like now to introduce the President and Chief Executive Officer of eTernity, Ms. Alison Prue. Ms. Prue… ?"

Alison was slated to speak twice. Now, at the beginning of the call, and later—after three of her VPs had provided more detail and elaboration on her statement, she was to return and present the company's financial predictions. On the organizer's advice, these were saved until last because the callers might drop off and start publishing the news.

Alison did as she was told. She read the script with as much freshness and brio as she could to make it sound as if she were speaking off the cuff. No one believed that, of course, but they were no doubt relieved not to have to listen to a droning recitation. She then deftly made the introductions and the hand-off to her vice-presidents—and turned off the microphone to her headset.

The next part of the call would take about twenty-five minutes. She sat back, pulled out her Blackberry, and began searching through any Tweets being posted on the presentation so far. She found one from the analyst from Goldman Sachs. It read: "*Evrybdy hot on eTY but v2.0 rumord late If dont hit 38c trouble*"

Alison felt her face flush. She flipped through the pages of the script to her second presentation to confirm her fears. There: 36 cents per share. Shit. And no mention of version 2.0 at all, just more upgrades of 1.0. *They're going to kill us,* she realized.

She stared at the page for a long time. Beside her, COO and VP of marketing Lawrence Kessler was delivering his share of the speech in his lapidary style. The others at the table were following along. Alison took the pen and notepad that had been placed before her on the table and marked the script. No one else noticed.

It was again time for her to read her part. The other executives, relieved to be done, barely followed along. But when, in the midst of reading the financials, she announced "38 cents per share," every one of them—and Tipo as well—snapped their heads back, and began to tear through their script. "What the fuck?" Kessler silently mouthed to Court Tanaka, the R&D director across from him. Tanaka shrugged and shook his head in disbelief.

By the time the question period began, the room was audibly rattled. When one of the questions was addressed to the usually unflappable Kessler, his answer was distracted and rambling. It was even worse with the others, especially CFO Vanesh Jayaram, who now seemed reluctant to speak at all. And it only got worse when, in response to a question about version 2.0 from the analyst at Merrill Lynch, Alison unhesitatingly guaranteed that it would be introduced by the end of the next quarter.

The instant the phone call was finished, Alison stood, tore off and headset and tossed it on the table. "Gentlemen," she announced, "you've now got your number and your delivery date. Now, *meet them*. We're playing for the win."

She stormed out of the boardroom, leaving the other executives to stare at each other in disbelief. "What the hell just happened?" Kessler demanded.

"She changed the numbers on us," whispered Jayaram. "How could she do that? Those were real numbers."

"How are we going to get two more cents?" asked Robinson Westerfield, the new director of manufacturing.

"She doesn't care how," said Tanaka. "I think she just told us that."

"Well, God help us," said Kessler. "If we don't hit those numbers the stock market is going to kill us. If we do, it'll take some fancy bookkeeping. And what if the auditors spot it?"

"Just pray they don't," said Westerfield. "Vanesh, that's your problem. I'll be taking the shot if we don't ship in time. We may end up sending out DOA products for a couple weeks. Good luck with that PR nightmare, Larry."

Jayaram rubbed his temples with his fingers. "Why is she doing this?"

"Maybe she wants to pump the stock to sell some of her shares."

"For what? This company is her life."

"Then she's building a war chest to go after Validator for the whole thing."

"God, I hate entrepreneurs," said Larry Kessler.

V. 9.0

D an checked his watch as he walked down the hall. Five minutes late. Shit. He'd let that customer call go too long. Well, he told himself, the board can hardly blame me for tending to business. Donna, who was manning the desk outside the boardroom, jumped to her feet and reached for the handle to one of the big mahogany double doors. "They've just started," she whispered and pulled open the door.

The board of directors, fourteen well dressed, gray-haired business Alphas representing the usual cross-section of race, gender, and industry sectors were precisely arrayed around the long table. They had all turned to listen to the imposing figure holding forth at the far end.

"You see," said Cosmo Validator, "there are times when you need to cull out the old male. They've done their job; they've bred with all of the females and left their genetic imprint on the next generation. Now you need new blood, otherwise the herd deteriorates." He put both hands on the polished table. "That's why sometimes, even when there's an impressive young male sniffing around, maybe even trophy-quality, you still shoot the old leader." He looked up into Dan's eyes. "It's the responsible thing to do."

Then Cosmo smiled and held out his arms. "Well, gentlemen," he announced, "now that our CEO has arrived, shall we begin our meeting?"

V. 9.1

The building was familiar. But it had been years—decades—since Dan had last driven in the Lockheed Business Park. It was one of those backwaters of Silicon Valley, an address that had once been the most exciting place to work on the planet. But the technology—and the type of building needed to house that technology—had moved onto Milpitas, Gilroy, Bangalore, and Shanghai. Now the streets and parking lots were nearly empty, the concrete tilt-up buildings gray and worn. The few remaining businesses were the anonymous also-rans and never-will-be's.

As he pulled into the driveway, he counted eleven cars in the parking lot, all huddled near the entrance—most of them Hondas and Toyotas… except for one incongruous Bentley whose unlikely presence made him chuckle.

As he stepped out of his car, the glass doors opened. Out stepped Armstrong Givens, dressed in jeans and an untucked dress shirt.

"In mufti, I see," said Dan as they shook hands.

"Obviously," said Armstrong. "But, of course, I'm only kidding myself. The Bentley is a complete giveaway."

"Think of it as a motivator," said Dan. "If they pull this off, they'll each drive one."

"Good lord, don't tell *them* that. Wait until they're done."

Dan looked around. "Nice pick. Even I couldn't imagine you out here." He studied the building some more. "Do I know this place?"

Armstrong laughed. "You don't recognize it? It's the old Atari headquarters."

"Okay, yeah. I remember when I first started working in the Valley, somebody gave me a tour and pointed this place out to me. Don't think I've ever been inside."

"Well, this place is like Memory Lane for me. Crazy company, Atari. Especially under Bushnell. We sold a lot of chips to those guys. So did Validator. That's one reason I picked it, right under Cosmo's nose. I'm hiding in plain sight."

"Atari. Pong. I think that's the first time I ever heard of Silicon Valley."

"Oh, this place fairly drips Valley history." He turned and pointed. "See that parking lot over there? That's where Steve Ross's helicopter touched down. After Warners bought Atari, Ross and his entourage decided that the Valley was too small-time for them to stay in. So they booked a hotel in the City and then took a chopper down here. They landed in the parking lot there, and then a limousine drove them the last 300 feet to the front door."

"You're kidding."

"Nope. It was like the biggest fuck-you imaginable by the Manhattan aristos to the Valley peasants. Ever wonder why you got such a cold shoulder when you came out from New York?"

Dan laughed. "After all these years. And I thought it was just me."

"Now you know. Anyway, we got our revenge. Within ten years, Manhattan was kissing our ass, begging us for money."

"Okay, now *that* part I remember," said Dan.

Inside, the building still seemed abandoned. The hallway floors were dirty, there were stains on the walls, and several of the offices they passed looked like they had been sealed in the last century. But one big room was brightly lit, and as they passed, Dan glanced in through the double glass doors to see a vast space filled with low cubicles and busy young men and women sitting at computer screens.

"Is that the crew?"

"Yes," Armstrong said over his shoulder, without breaking stride.

"Am I going to meet them?"

"I'd prefer not."

"Why not?"

Armstrong stopped walking. "Because enough of them know who you are by sight, and your presence will only confuse them—and that could lead to crazy ideas like this being a Validator Software project. For now, I want them to keep thinking that I'm just an eccentric millionaire."

"Which is, of course, true…"

"Also, you don't want to find out later that Asperger's is contagious. We can talk in my office."

They entered a huge room with exposed overhead ductwork and walls painted matte black. A single military surplus gray steel desk sat in the center of the room, with an expensive leather executive chair behind it. The desk and chair were flanked by two antique floor lamps with Tiffany stained glass shades. There were stacks of papers on the floor behind the desk. A rope of bundled cables ran from the computers and phones on the desk across the floor and disappeared into the shadows.

"Very nice," said Dan.

"Isn't it? Sort of *Scarface* meets *1984*, wouldn't you say?"

"Cheery, too. Why did you pick this office?"

Armstrong dragged a straight-backed steel chair from a dark corner of the room, put it in front of the desk, and gestured for Dan to sit. "A lot of reasons. Because it keeps me mysterious to the troops. Because it ensures absolute privacy. Because I've disconnected the smoke detector—and most of all, because I'm tapping into the most powerful juju in Silicon Valley outside of the Packard garage."

Dan slumped as far as he could against the rigid seatback. "Oh? Do tell."

"You don't recognize it, Mr. Crowen, because you weren't here, but in the late 1970s, this was the very epicenter of the electronics world. This was the Game Room, where Nolan Bushnell and his motley crew set up all the prototypes of their new arcade games and invited young gamers to come and play them for free."

"I see..."

"No you don't. Not yet. Because one of that crew was Steve Jobs, and one of the gamers he invited in was his buddy Steve Wozniak. So as much as anywhere in the world, this is where Apple began as well." Armstrong jabbed his forefinger straight down on the desktop. "Right here. Ground zero. This is where both the video game and the personal computer industries begin. We're talking a trillion dollars a year. I'll settle for one thousandth of that."

Dan laughed. "So, you are invoking the Great Digital Gods? I never knew you were such a superstitious old fool."

Armstrong laughed with him. "Well, two out of the three. In fact, when I told the kids out there about this room, they almost crossed themselves and genuflected. Don't forget, Dan, the insufferable pricks of one generation are the benevolent immortals to the next." His face suddenly darkened. "And speaking of life and death, how is your career doing these days? Are you still breathing?"

"Just barely," said Dan. "I'm on life support. I assume that Validator is already talking to the board without me."

"I see."

"So, in light of that, are you going to hit our target date? Because I may be down to days, even hours."

Armstrong spun away, then rose from his chair and began to pace across the shadowy floor behind his desk. Then he returned, put his fists on the desk, and leaned forward. "Daniel," he said, "let me ask you something. Are you sure you don't want to go it alone? You give me the word and in six months I'll have a finished product without the Validator kernel. You and I have got the dough. And, shit, if we need more, we can get secret meetings with a half-a-dozen venture capitalists *today*."

He leaned closer. "We could build one great company, you and me. Hell, I feel so liberated these days, it's like I've Come Out a second time. You've brought me back to where I'm the most happy. So come on, Dan, fuck all of that big business bullshit. Let's go it alone."

Dan shook his head. "I'm sorry, Arm, but as fun as that sounds, it won't work. We'd spend the rest of our careers fighting off Validator lawsuits. No, we do this one in-house."

Armstrong Givens frowned, then nodded. "All right, my friend, you're the boss. At least I'm not slinging hash anymore."

Dan smiled feebly. "Better start praying to those Digital Gods of yours."

"Pray? Hell, I'm going to start sacrificing virgins. There's got to be a few of them down the hall."

V. 9.2

The meeting had started badly and gotten worse. Through each of the six presentations by her executive team, Alison had sat uncharacteristically silent. That, plus her pale face and set jaw, had made each presenter in turn increasingly jumpy and hesitant. They had known coming in that they were going to be delivering bad news—that with seven days left before the end of the quarter, eTernity was not going to hit the numbers Alison had promised the analysts, and Version 2.0 was continuing to slip—but they couldn't read her response. Was this angry acceptance or the prelude to an explosion? By the time the last presenter, poor Vanesh Jayaram, began laying out the financial situation at the firm, his hands were shaking visibly.

He finished at last and slumped back with visible relief. No one spoke; nor did anyone look at the CEO. Finally, Alison took the sheaf of papers she held in her hand and dismissively tossed them on the table. She looked around at all of the bowed faces and lowered eyes and said, "2.0 comes out in forty-five days."

"It's still really buggy, Alison," said Court Tanaka delicately.

"Forty five days, Court. If we have to, we'll ship it with the bugs and patch later."

"That's risky."

She ignored him. "Forty-five days. And we start leaking the intro date, starting now."

"And earnings?" asked Larry Kessler.

"We will hit our numbers, no matter what."

"How?" he asked. "You saw the numbers. They speak for themselves."

"And I speak for this company," she replied. "Book some of the sales from next quarter."

"We already have. It's not enough. Anything more will attract attention."

"Then temporarily lay off people. We'll take our numbers off the top."

"It's too late. And if we announce a lay-off, we'll still take a stock hit."

Alison's eyes flared. She looked around the table. "I can't begin to tell you how disappointed I am in all of you," she said. "This company used to do the impossible."

"Yeah," said Kessler. "But that was before our CEO started pulling financials out of a top hat."

Alison turned in her chair and spoke directly to him. "Alright, Larry, you're the Chief *Operations* Officer. What do we do? What are our choices?"

Kessler looked at the others, then back at his CEO. "At this point, we're down to just two. One, we keep pushing, and try to get as close to your target as we can. We take the stock hit—and pray the SEC doesn't show up at our door. Or two, we immediately send out a press advisory announcing an adjustment in our predictions—and take the stock hit now."

"In other words," said Alison dismissively, "we look either crooked or incompetent. Is that it?"

"Basically, yes."

There was a quick knock on the door. Daisy, Alison's new secretary, peeked around. "I'm very sorry to interrupt, Ms. Prue, but Mr. Bellflower is on the phone. He says it's important."

Great timing, Arthur. Alison nodded glumly. "I'll take it in my office." Leaving the papers on the table, she rose. "Gentlemen, I'll have an answer for you by day's end." She glared at the secretary taking notes. "Stop writing. *Now.*" She turned and looked around the table. "I want you all to sit in here and come up with every trick you can think of to get us within range of our prediction. *Every* trick. Not just the half-assed efforts you've come up with so far. Act like your careers depend upon it—because they do. We'll reconvene at 2:00 p.m."

She closed her office door behind her, leaned with her back against it, and burst into tears. Wiping them away, she composed herself, walked to her desk, and picked up the phone.

"Arthur?"

"We have an appointment," Bellflower said flatly. "A car will pick you up at 4:00 p.m. to take you to SFO."

"Where are we going?"

"I'll explain in the plane. Don't worry about clothes; you'll be home by midnight."

"Arthur, I'm incredibly busy today."

"You're about to get busier."

V. 9.3

D an looked out the window at the private jets parked in front of the San Jose Jetport. Enjoy the view, he told himself, you aren't going to see it again for a long, long time.

"It's good to have you on board again, Mr. Crowen," said Andrea, the attendant, looking exactly the same as she always did. "It's been what—six months—since the last time you were our guest?"

"I guess it has been," he said. "After all those busy months, you probably enjoyed the break."

Andrea smiled dreamily. "Oh, Mr. Validator has managed to keep us all on the run in the meantime."

"I suppose he has."

"May I get you anything before we take off?"

Dan took a deep breath. "I know it's a little early, but how about one of your famous mile-high martinis?"

"I'll get right on it."

Dan sat back and looked around the cabin, marking it in his mind. You read about it in novels, he thought, but it isn't very often that real life comes full circle. But here I am. Off to Idaho to once again have my life turned upside down by Cosmo Validator. He smiled. Or maybe this time it's right side up...

He heard the ice tinkling in the cocktail shaker. Beneath him, he felt the brakes release and the plane begin to taxi forward. The view outside the window started to slide. Dan pulled his phone out of his briefcase and dialed home.

Annabelle answered.

"I've been summoned," he told her.

She sighed. "So," she asked, "is this it?"

"Yeah, I'm pretty sure it is."

"Well, honey, there are worse things. We've certainly learned that lately."

"Yes, we have."

"How do you feel?"

"You know, Annie, I've been dreading this moment for my entire adult life. And now that it's here, I'm actually kind of relieved. And ready. I don't think I've ever been so weary."

"I know, baby," she said. Dan could hear the tears in her voice. "When you get home tonight, we'll have a late dinner. We'll sleep in. And when you're ready we'll talk about getting away to someplace quiet and restful."

"I like it all."

Andrea set the martini down in front of him. Dan mouthed 'thanks' and turned back to the phone. "You know, Annabelle, my only real regret is that I didn't get that skunkworks project done in time. We were so close."

"Listen," she said, "you can walk away now knowing that despite everything, you saved your company. Everyone else will see that soon enough. As for the skunkworks, it doesn't have to die. You once told me that no good idea ever really goes away around here. It just goes dormant until it's needed."

"Did I say that? Then it's probably not true."

"Let Armstrong run with the thing. With you out of the picture, he can probably get away with it. He's more than clever enough to cut a deal with Validator. You were the real problem. Once you're gone, the conflict of interest is gone, too. I'll bet you Validator Software buys Armstrong out in six months. And Arm'll take care of you, because he's always been a man of honor."

Dan chuckled. "You should have been a businesswoman, baby."

"It's all those years being married to you. And I'll bet you've already thought of all of this."

"Yes, but not so succinctly. Still, we can't make any final decisions until I know what my termination package will be. They'll probably want to keep me around for the transition. Or maybe Cosmo already has my replacement waiting in the wings. Either way, I'll likely know in about three hours."

"Call me afterwards, will you?"

"You know I will."

"And after you nobly shake Cosmo's hand and thank him for everything, please tell him from me that I think he should go fuck himself."

Dan laughed out loud. "Oh, it'll be my pleasure."

V. 9.4

Alison Prue and Arthur Bellflower, in their rented jet, were already flying over Mt. Lassen. Alison finally reached across the aisle, tapped the man on the arm, and said, "Okay, Arthur. Are you ready now to tell me where we're going?"

Bellflower, who had been dozing—or at least pretending to—opened his eyes. "You know, young lady, there's an old saying in Silicon Valley. It's that eventually you will work with, for, or against everyone else in this town."

"I think I heard that somewhere."

"Now, tell me, Alison, how much do you know about my background?"

"You mean, beyond what I read on Wikipedia? Can I trust that source?"

Bellflower ignored her. "For example, to illustrate that saying, did you know that way back, when I quit National Semiconductor and started Reason Software, my very first angel investor—the very first investor who believed in me, not as a corporate executive but as an honest-to-god entrepreneur—was Cosmo Validator?"

Alison froze. "No, I didn't know that. Are you still in touch with him?"

"Remember when I told you about my old friends?" he asked her. "Cosmo is the godfather of my children. And he was there for the christening of both my grandchildren. We have lunch about once a month."

Good god, she thought. "Is that where we're going, Arthur? Are we going to see Validator? Where's his ranch—Idaho? Utah?"

"...And when I started Reason, do you know what banker gave me my first line of credit?"

"I have no idea."

"Dan Crowen."

Alison's eyes narrowed. "Don't tell me you regularly have lunch with him, too."

"I haven't seen him in ten years."

"What are you trying to tell me, Arthur?" Alison asked.

Bellflower put his two index fingers to his lips, as if in thought. "Only that, the more years go by, the more I'm convinced of the truth of that old saying."

V. 9.5

As always, Virgil Mason was waiting for him at Validator's private hangar at the Coeur d'Alene airport. "No bags?" he asked as Dan came down the steps.

"Not this time," said Dan. "Going home tonight."

They spoke little on the long drive, this time under a low sun glowing through piled clouds. When they pulled up in front of the big ranch house, Mason reached over and shook Dan's hand. "Good luck, Mr. Crowen. When you're ready to go I'll be waiting out here."

Mary Mason opened the big front door. She had changed her hair, letting it turn a striking silver-gray. It seemed to underscore the time that had passed. "Hey, stranger," she said and wrapped him in a hug. When she pulled back, there were tears in her eyes.

"It's been too long again," said Dan.

She nodded. "They're all waiting for you in Mr. Validator's office."

"They?"

"I'm supposed to take you up there."

Dan nodded. "Everything well with you?"

A tear broke and slid down Mary's right cheek. She put a hand up too late to catch it. "As good as can be expected."

They walked silently through the house. Apart from a few more Remingtons and Russells, the great hall was unchanged. Beyond the giant window, the snow-covered mountains were the palest of oranges. Mary led him up a half-dozen steps and on into Cosmo's private wing. In all the years he'd known Cosmo, Dan had never once been invited to this part of the house. *Well,* he thought, *at least this is something.*

After passing an exercise room, a gun room, and a sauna, they stopped at a pair of cedar doors under a large pediment of the same wood, all of it carved with acanthus leaves, rosettes, and oak leaves. In the center of one door, carved in a rococo medallion, was an ornate "C," and on the other was a "V." *No font of holy water?* Dan asked himself grimly.

Mary reached for the handle to the right door. She kissed him on the cheek and whispered, "Good luck," then opened the door.

Dan found himself at the threshold of a surprisingly large room, filled with hunting trophies, awards and photographs, and all the other accoutrements of fame. Through the far window, he could see the sun blazing over distant mountains and a wide valley; its light reflected endlessly off the gold, silver, cut glass, and polished wooden objects in the room.

A silhouette, its corona of hair gleaming white, rose in front of the sunlight and threw a shadow towards him across a huge mahogany desk. "Come in Dan," said Cosmo Validator. He pointed behind Dan's right shoulder. "Shall I make the introductions?"

Dan turned... and was surprised to see Alison Prue and Arthur Bellflower sitting on an oxblood leather Chesterfield sofa. Both of them rose.

"Good to see you again, Dan," said Bellflower, stepping forward to shake Dan's hand. "It's been a very long time."

"It has, Arthur. And what an unlikely place for a reunion."

Bellflower nodded. "It is indeed." He turned. "Please allow me to introduce you to Ms. Alison Prue."

Dan swallowed hard as he stepped forward to take Alison's hand. Her grip was cold but strong. "Alison, it's a pleasure to finally meet you after all this time."

"The pleasure is all mine—I think," she said.

"And Dan," Validator went on, with only a trace of amusement in his voice. "I'm sure you remember my assistant, Lisa Holmes." He made a casual gesture to the figure sitting in a chair by the desk, to his left.

"Yes," said Daniel evenly. He made a crisp nod in the woman's direction. "Ms. Holmes."

"It's like a family reunion," said Validator with a wry smile.

As if on cue, the sun dipped behind a cloud, dimming the glare and throwing Cosmo's face into relief for the first time. "Please, everyone, join me here and be seated. This won't take long. I'm afraid I have another appointment—with the governor—after this. And I'm sure you will all want to get home before it gets too late."

They each found seats. Dan's chair had steer horns for arms; Alison's was upholstered in zebra. Bellflower sat on a small Grecian couch along the right wall under a large George Catlin painting of Indian warriors spearing buffalo in the snow.

Validator waited for everyone to make themselves comfortable. Finally he said, "I'll make this simple. We already have a general agreement in place between the two boards." He nodded to the man on the couch. "Thank you, Arthur, for staying on at eTernity after the IPO."

Alison turned to stare at Bellflower. He didn't return the look.

"Obviously," Validator continued, "this will need shareholder approval. And there's no way we can escape the SEC taking a good hard look…"

It suddenly hit Dan what was about to happen. "Oh my God," he whispered.

"…but I think that with Validator Software increasingly uncompetitive and its stock near its historic low, there shouldn't be much of a problem."

"Problem with what?" asked Alison.

"The merger," Validator said calmly. "Your company is going to buy mine, with the merged company to be called Validator Corporation."

"We don't need you," protested Alison. Her voice rose. "We're already running your company into the ground, Mr. Validator."

Cosmo waited patiently. "In fact, you *do* need us," he said. "For one thing, Ms. Prue, you are increasingly out of your depth—as was illustrated by that foolish and impetuous prediction you made to the analysts last week. Your company is about to take a devastating stock hit, you may be investigated by the Justice Department for fraud, and your senior management is on the brink of mutiny. You're a very talented businesswoman, young lady, but you need adult supervision until you're ready to run a great company— and I'd prefer not to lose you in the process."

Alison's face turned red. She spun towards Bellflower, nearly coming out her chair. "Arthur, you agree with this?"

"It was my idea," said Bellflower calmly.

Why, if *we* are buying *them*, are we taking *their* name?"

"Because," Cosmo interrupted, "it is a distinguished name, and as old as our industry. Or, if you prefer, because it will give your company the gravity it currently lacks."

"I don't believe this is happening!" Alison shouted. She gave each of the men a furious look in turn. "It's as if, after everything, I have *no* say in this decision."

Bellflower held up his open hands to calm her. "As you well know, Alison, your say in a matter like this is determined entirely by your shareholdings in the firm."

Though he had not yet said a word, Dan was no less stunned than Alison. It had already struck him that his termination was one of the cards yet to be played in this plan. Trying to act confident, he asked, "How long have you been planning this, Cosmo?"

Validator smiled, but chose not to answer him directly. "The good news is that this merger is almost a perfect fit, with little redundancy, so we won't have to suffer the bad publicity of lay-offs and all the other complications."

"So that's why you killed my sales force," Dan said with a mixture of anger and admiration. "You've been planning this for three years, haven't you?"

Cosmo's face went blank. "You of all people should know how erratic and unpredictable I am, Dan. I hardly know what I'm doing tomorrow, much less next week. But I can assure you that all my actions have been in the best interests of the firm and its shareholders."

"Oh yes," Dan replied wryly. "Let the official record show that."

Alison turned again to Bellflower, this time as if the two of them were alone. "Arthur," she said urgently, "we don't need these people. I screwed up, I admit it, but we'll weather it. There's nothing Validator Software can give us that we don't already have."

"Actually, that's not true," said Cosmo, picking up a piece of paper and glancing at it. "Leaving aside our $6 billion in annual revenues, profit margins that are higher than yours, and 20,000 loyal customers—remarkably loyal, given the last couple years—there is also the matter of new products. Arthur tells me you'll be lucky to get your next generation product out just six months late. Meanwhile, Dan here has a little skunkworks operation going in Santa Clara—run by your old friend Armstrong Givens, Ms. Prue—that's not only got a superior product to yours, but is going to beat you to market. How long until it's ready, Dan?"

"Six weeks."

Validator turned to the figure beside him. "Is that what your intelligence says, Lisa?"

"More or less," she said, flicking through a report on her laptop.

Dan started to laugh. He clapped his hands four times, each clap louder than the last. "Well played, Cosmo. After all these years, you can still surprise me." He began to rise from his chair. "Well, good luck to you all. Shall I have Virgil drive me back to the airport?"

"Not just yet," said Cosmo. "Please sit down, Dan. We still have a personnel matter to attend to."

Dan reluctantly did as he was asked.

Cosmo folded his hands on the desk. He didn't speak for a long time, as if what he was about to say was difficult and needed to be carefully phrased.

Finally he spoke. "Dan, I've concluded that, after nearly fifty years, it's time for me to retire from the electronics industry. As you know, my wife Amber is currently the president of the Idaho Chamber of Commerce. She's now decided to run for Congress from the 2nd District. I have it on good authority that she will win, too," he said with a wink.

"Because of that, I plan to spend the next few years working in Washington, out of my Georgetown townhouse. By coincidence," he said, smiling knowingly at Bellflower, "Arthur and I will be asked by the President of the United States to serve on his Council of Science and Technology Advisors, of which I will be the chairman. Of course, that's not yet public news, so please keep it to yourselves."

Dan grinned. "Does the President know this yet?"

Validator laughed. "No, not yet."

"Then, Cosmo," said Dan, "let me be the first to congratulate you and your wife on this triumph of the democratic process."

"Thank you," said Validator. "The people have spoken—or at least they will in November. And that brings me to you, Dan. Arthur and I have concluded, and both of our boards have agreed, to offer you the chairmanship of the newly merged Validator Software."

Cosmo then turned to Alison. "We have also agreed to offer you, Ms. Prue, the position of chief executive officer of the new company."

Cosmo Validator stood without waiting for a response. The others followed suit. "I will expect a response from both of you in the next forty-eight hours. In the meantime, while we're getting the cars ready to take you to the airport, shall we retire to the living room to celebrate? I have champagne prepared."

V. 9.6

The quartet walked out of the office in pairs: Alison with Bellflower, Dan with Validator. When Cosmo got a step ahead, Dan glanced back to see that Lisa Holmes hadn't followed them. She had already turned her back to the departing group to talk on her cell phone.

"After all this double dealing behind my back," Alison hissed to Bellflower, "why should I even consider taking this offer?"

"Because," he replied, "it'll still be the company you built, and you can't let it fail now right on the brink of such a huge success. And because it will make you one of the most powerful businesswomen in the world. Got anything better planned?"

Dan caught Validator's arm and stopped him. "I was doing a great job for you, Cosmo," he said. "Why did you put me through this hell?"

Validator pulled himself to his full height. "Because," he said, "you were a brilliant CEO of a mature company. But this business is changing fast. And if I was going to let you be the chairman of a company with my name on it, by God, I was going to make sure you knew how to think like an entrepreneur. You needed to be tested... just like young Miss Prue up there needed to learn how to be like you."

"You should have trusted me."

"I do, Dan. I've just given you the only thing in my life that I've ever really cared about. Isn't that enough?"

A small, folding campaign table had been set up the middle of the great hall. It bore a champagne bucket in a towel and a silver tray with four glass flutes. The four of them encircled it. "This was John C. Fremont's field desk," said Cosmo. "Just imagine him and Kit Carson standing here, preparing to go off the map and conquer a new world." He filled the glasses, handing each in turn to the others. Then he filled and raised his own glass.

Bellflower raised his glass as well. "A toast," he said, "to the new Validator Software and the two people who will run it. May you be both smart and lucky."

"And," added Cosmo Validator, "may you never let them see the strings."

V. 9.7

Bellflower and Validator were lost in conversation about children, grandchildren, and fishing expeditions. Dan walked out onto the big stone patio. The mountain peaks were now a deep orange, their bases turning gray-blue. Above, the setting sun had turned the sky and clouds blood red, streaked with flames.

He was joined by Alison Prue. Together, they stared silently at the vista.

"How did you manage to recruit Armstrong?" Alison asked.

"I gave him the one thing he really wanted."

"What? Money? Stock? He had those."

"No," said Dan, "I gave him himself."

"How good is that new product?"

"Good enough."

Alison stared at him for a moment, then looked back to the sunset. "We beat you. None of this changes any of that. We beat you fair and square."

Dan started to tell her that not a single word of that last sentence was true. But he caught himself. He was Alison's boss now, her mentor. They were now in this together. "Yes," he told her. "Yes, you did."

THE END

Also Available from Michael S. Malone

The Virtual Corporation

The Microprocessor: A Biography

Intellectual Capital

One Digital Day

Infinite Loop

Valley of Heart's Delight

Bill & Dave

The Future Arrived Yesterday

Four Percent

The Guardian of All Things

Coming Soon From Michael S. Malone

Trinity: The History of Intel Corporation

MICHAEL S. MALONE is one of the world's best-known technology writers. He has covered Silicon Valley and high-tech for more than 25 years, beginning with the *San Jose Mercury News* as the nation's first daily high-tech reporter, where he was twice nominated for the Pulitzer Prize for investigative reporting. His articles and editorials have appeared in such publications as *The Wall Street Journal*, *The Economist* and *Fortune*, and for two years he was a columnist for *The New York Times*.

He was editor of *Forbes ASAP*, the world's largest-circulation business-tech magazine, at the height of the dot-com boom. Malone is the author or co-author of nearly twenty award-winning books, notably the best-selling *The Virtual Corporation, Bill & Dave*, and *The Future Arrived Yesterday*. Malone has also hosted three nationally syndicated public television interview series and co-produced the Emmy-nominated primetime PBS miniseries on social entrepreneurs, "The New Heroes."

As an entrepreneur, Malone was a founding shareholder of eBay, Siebel Systems (sold to Oracle) and Qik (sold to Skype), and is currently a co-founder and director of new start-up PatientKey Inc. Malone holds an MBA from Santa Clara University, where he is currently an adjunct professor. He is also an associate fellow of the Said Business School at Oxford University, and is a Distinguished Friend of Oxford.

ABOUT
BARKING RAIN PRESS

D id you know that six media conglomerates publish eighty percent of the books in the United States? As the publishing industry continues to contract, opportunities for emerging and mid-career authors are drying up. Who will write the literature of the twenty-first century if just a handful of profit-focused corporations are left to decide who—and what—is worthy of publication?

Barking Rain Press is dedicated to the creation and promotion of thoughtful and imaginative contemporary literature, which we believe is essential to a vital and diverse culture. As a nonprofit organization, Barking Rain Press is an independent publisher that seeks to cultivate relationships with new and mid-career writers over time, to be thorough in the editorial process, and to make the publishing process an experience that will add to an author's development—and ultimately enhance our literary heritage.

In selecting new titles for publication, Barking Rain Press considers authors at all points in their careers. Our goal is to support the development of emerging and mid-career authors—not just single books—as we know from experience that a writer's audience is cultivated over the course of several books.

Support for these efforts comes primarily from the sale of our publications; we also hope to attract grant funding and private donations. Whether you are a reader or a writer, we invite you to take a stand for independent publishing and become more involved with Barking Rain Press. With your support, we can make sure that talented writers thrive, and that their books reach the hands of spirited, curious readers. Find out more at our website.

Barking Rain Press

WWW.BARKINGRAINPRESS.ORG

ALSO FROM BARKING RAIN PRESS

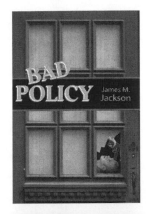

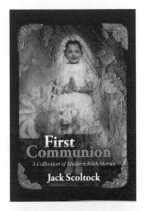

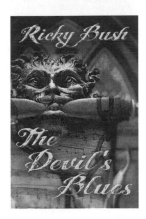

READ 4 CHAPTERS OF EACH BOOK AT OUR WEBSITE

Made in the USA
San Bernardino, CA
11 December 2013